Love Through the Eyes of a Fifteen Year Old

I0629906

Author
Anonymous

Love Through The Eyes of a Fifteen Year Old

The characters and the story in this book are fiction.

www.chelseasongbird.com

Printed in the United States of America

Copyright© 2009 by **CHELSEASONGBIRD PUBLISHING CO.**

Library of Congress Control Number: 2010901164
ISBN 978-0-587-04877-0

My inspiration to write this book came
from a fifteen year old, and her friends.
Therefore I dedicate this book to:

Britty Rae

Introduction

This book is about a fifteen year old who knows the love of a family, and the love of friends. Two very different loves, yet one is as strong as the other. This fifteen year old learns that the most important love is the love of one's self. You must love and nourish yourself in order to love others. This is displayed throughout the book. Hope you enjoy your read.

Acknowledgments

This book was a joy to write. The intent of this book is to strengthen the beliefs and lifestyles of future generations of the United States of America. Britty Rae, who asked questions about why we need so many laws, has some of her questions answered in this book: politicians wishing to make a name for themselves or just needing to look like they are doing their jobs, or money talks. I don't believe our forefathers ever meant for there to be so many laws.

Table of Contents

Chapter 1
Let Me Introduce Myself

My name is Chelsea Songbird and I belong to the Cherokee Nation. This summer the family went to Washington D.C. to see the Washington Monument. The Cherokee tribe contributed a block to the Washington Monument that reads, "Cherokee Nation 1850." My parents wanted the family to see that the Cherokee Nation has a presence in Washington and we have a voice in our country that speaks loud and clear. The family always takes a vacation in the summer and this just happened to be one that had an education tied in with a lot of fun.

The whole family takes its heritage seriously. Our heritage has been passed down from the preceding Cherokee generations to keep it alive. My father speaks the Cherokee language fluently and shares it with the family. We all know words and phrases, but not like dad does.

The vacation this summer was picked by my dad, and not that I don't appreciate it or anything, but it was his pick and not mine. I know with age, my appreciation will increase, but this summer vacation felt like a history class.

Summer vacation is a very important part of our lives. We save our money all year so we can have a blast for two marvelous weeks out of the year. After all, my parents work hard to pay for our home, cars, and to put food on the table all year long. I struggle to make good grades so some day I can have a good job and provide for my family when I have one. We all deserve the highest and best kind of quality vacation we can save for.

Because we save so much money each month, summer vacation stays on our mind all year long. Every time I put money in my piggy bank, I think about what a great time I'm going to have with it. That makes it easier to save all year long. I get to pick next year's vacation spot and it will be in Florida. I want to spend all my time on the beach and in the water. I have researched Florida in the library and I think Pensacola is where I want to go.

I'm turning fifteen this summer, July 25, so my parents promised me more freedom so I can get used to being responsible for myself. After all, by the time I'm sixteen I will have a car and a real part-time job. Right now, I get an allowance for cleaning the house and mowing the lawn. It's not a lot of money but it makes for a great vacation.

Not that I'm wishing my life away, but I dream about having more freedom to do what I want when I want. I totally agree with my parents on the idea of giving me more freedom before I'm sixteen to see how I handle it. They promised me my own room next year on our Florida vacation. Just the thought of getting out of bed when I want, going to bed when I want, and just the freedom of having my own room thrills my soul and sends quivers through my body. I feel a sudden intense emotion when I think about being on the beach in my two-piece bathing suit with my newly developing body. I have just started developing breasts; you know, the mammary gland that surfaces on the body between the neck and the abdomen. This is a sure sign I'm growing up. By next summer, I suppose they will double in size. The first things I plan to buy with my savings are a beach towel, swimming suit, and big floppy hat that ties under the chin. I'm more excited about next year's vacation than any of them we have taken so far.

The airplane ride from Washington D.C. back to my home in Tahlequah, Oklahoma was a bumpy experience. We ran into some wind that caused us to knock against each other, even though we were belted into our seats. We all began to pray for our safety. My heart was beating like it would come out of my chest. All I could think of was that I was too young to die. I asked God to forgive me for my sins that I might have forgotten to ask forgiveness for. I then told God I still had a lot of good to do on earth and that if He would spare this plane He would be impressed with my works. About this time we hit a pocket of wind that knocked two airline attendants to the floor. I was sitting between my mom and dad and they each grabbed one of my hands and we began to tell each other how much we loved one another. The pilot then came on the loud speaker and said, "We have clear skies in fifty miles, so everyone brace yourself because we have some more wind turbulence until we make the fifty-mile mark. Try to relax; you are in good hands." About this time, one of the airline attendants asked if we needed a blanket or pillow. My mom asked her if she was all right because we had seen her take a nasty fall. She let us know everything was okay and that was not the first time she had fallen on a flight. My mom then said, "A blanket would be nice; it might help my daughter stop shaking." The stewardess then covered all three of us with the blanket.

There were a few more bumps and just as suddenly as the storm appeared, it disappeared. I guess these planes fly really fast. The sunshine was a welcome sight, and I could see the relief in my parents' eyes. Dad said, "There's the runway; we made it home." We all breathed a sigh of relief, and gave a group hug. The fear and anxiety is all behind us, and now I think we all have a greater appreciation for life. I'm talking about everyone on that flight and not just my family.

The drive back to Tahlequah, where our home is, was filled with exciting stories about our two-week vacation in Washington D.C. My dad said he will relish this trip for the rest of his life. That is, except for the traffic. The way the road layout is designed is enough to drive you crazy. I never saw so many one-way streets. I felt sorry for my dad driving in the congested traffic; he always gave a sigh of relief when we finally made it to our destination each day. He said if we ever go back to Washington D.C. we will definitely not rent a car; we will take public transit.

My mother was most impressed with the Capitol. It is the home of the Senate and the House of Representatives. We just happened to be there on a day when a live debate was taking place on the House or Senate floor. I think my dad had planned it that way. As a matter of fact, he made plans to visit the White House six months in advance. He contacted our Senator to help make his plans.

My dad talked a lot about the White House. He refers to it as the most famous house in America. The White House looks magical with the glow of hidden floodlights in the early evening. It's like a fairytale land. The eighteen and a half acres around the White House impressed me. All the flower gardens and the lush grassy lawn with the most beautiful magnolia tree I have ever seen was thought to have been planted by Andrew Jackson. We entered the White House from the east side of the house where from the Library we could see portraits of the first ladies. We then went through the Green Room where many American paintings hang on the walls. When we reached the Blue Room, I looked out the window and saw the beautiful Washington Monument; Presidents and their wives use the Blue Room to receive guests. The furniture in the Blue Room is the oldest original furniture in the White House collection. The Red Room had a portrait of Dolly Madison with many landscape paintings. Next we entered the State Dining Room where the President and First Lady entertain guests with dinner.

Yes, it was some house to see. Its address, 1600 Pennsylvania Avenue N.W., is known to people all over the world. The White House puts on a Fourth of July fireworks display like none anyone in the family has ever seen.

My favorite place is the National Monument. It is 555 feet tall and we went to the top where the observatory let us see Washington D.C. the way a bird flying high would see it. Knowing my ancestors contributed a block to the Washington Monument gave it meaning that touched my soul.

Across the Potomac River from the Capitol stands the Pentagon. It is a five-sided building that is the headquarters for the U.S. Armed Forces, the most costly organization in the world.

The most beautiful building I have ever seen in my life is the Washington National Cathedral. The rose window is made up of 10,500 pieces of stained glass. It is the sixth-largest cathedral in the world.

On the last day of our trip, we rented bikes to go down the Mount Vernon trail. On our bikes, we crossed over the Memorial Bridge from D.C. to hit the trail, which runs along the Potomac all the way to Mount Vernon. It truly is a sight to behold; if you ever visit Washington D.C., you must rent bikes and go down this gorgeous trail. Mount Vernon is the homeland of George Washington. It makes a bygone era come to life with its magnificent estate and hillside lawns. We packed our lunch – peanut butter and jelly – and had lunch on George Washington's land. It was truly the most peaceful and tranquil day of the entire vacation.

Washington D.C. is a great place to visit, but I was glad to see the highway sign that read, Tahlequah next exit. I was homesick.

We live in the country and the back of our property joins a wildlife refuge with streams, ponds, and lots of woods. I enjoy having access to the wildlife refuge and I sometimes feel like I own it. After all, no one can ever build on it and my dad only fenced our property on two sides, so it is an open pathway that seems never ending. My favorite spot is a pond with a large oak tree that extends out over the pond. On one of the limbs of the oak tree, my dad tied a heavy-gauged rope so we could all swing out to the deep part of the pond to swim. It is one of my favorite pastimes in the summer. As a matter of fact, it was the first thing I did when we got home. The middle of a July summer can be very hot in Oklahoma, and there is nothing like a big splash in a cold pond. There was not even a breath of wind and my parents could hear my splash in the water from the backyard. I yelled at them and said the water is great. Before I knew it, they joined me and we swam for at least an hour while the house was cooling down.

Suddenly, out of the corner of my eye I spotted Bam, a doe we had raised from a young dear, a fawn. We had fed Bam until she was old enough to take care of herself. A friend of ours found her in the woods all alone and gave her to me. At first, my parents objected because of the vegetable garden. They knew that Bam would have a feast on the tender potatoes and broccoli my mom planted. The solution to this problem was a solar hot wire. We put up three strands, and Bam only had to hit it once. I never knew a doe could jump so high. She never came near it again.

As I walked out of the water, Bam started walking toward me. The first thing she did was smell of my hands to see if I had a treat for her. I gave her a hug and I swear she was wrapping her neck around me to hug me back.

My dad goes deer hunting every year and we make chili out of the venison, the flesh of the deer. My dad teases me each year by saying if he doesn't shoot a deer we'll just have to eat Bam. He knows he can get a rile out of me. He would never harm a hair on Bam's head, or body. She is like part of the family.

Mom and dad were right behind me in giving Bam a big hug. She was as glad to see us as we were to see her. She was wagging her tail to let us know how elated she was that we were back. She kept walking around us and nudging us with her nose. It was a wonderful reunion.

Bam started walking toward the house knowing we would give her a sugar cube, which she has been missing for the past two weeks. When I opened the door to the house, Bam tried to come in. She's never been allowed in the house but always tries to push her way in anyway. She thinks she is family - well, she is family – but she still can't come in the house. I gave her a sugar cube and she was in heaven. I swear, her eyes got bigger and started twinkling.

We have an outdoor shower for when we swim in the pond. We use eco-friendly soap and keep bath robes within reach. We all took a quick shower and grabbed a lawn chair. The birds were singing as if to welcome us home.

The outdoor shower is one of my favorite things in the whole world. It sits under a large maple tree at the edge of the cement patio. It is made of cedar wood and my dad put a clear coat of sealer on the wood so it will last a lifetime. I can see my mom and dad's head and their legs up to the knee when they shower, but I'm not tall enough for people to see my head just yet. What I love about this outdoor shower is that I feel like I'm one with nature. We are the only creatures on earth who have to wear clothes. I have a great body, but would never run around outside naked, I guess because of what happened to Adam and Eve. They made it where I have to cover myself except in this outdoor shower. Being naked is okay because no one sees me but the birds and the bees.

Speaking of bees, one time when I was just six years old, and taking an outdoor shower, a bee joined me. I guess the bee wanted to take a shower with me, but I was horrified at it. I started swatting at this bee, which then started flying closer and much faster. I started screaming and, without a thought, ran out of the shower buck naked. My mom and dad and sister burst out laughing as I ran into the house leaving the still-running shower and, hopefully, the bee behind me. That bee hit the glass door and I finished my shower in the house. Mom later told me if I hadn't shown so much fear and hadn't swatted at that bee it probably wouldn't have even noticed me. Let's just say, I like the birds much more than the bees.

My sister's name is Cloie and we are very close. She's always included me in things she did, like going to the mall to shop for clothes and taking me to get an ice cream cone. She is just the greatest sister anyone could ask for. I missed her going on vacation with us this year. Cloie is an exchange student and is studying the French language at a university in Paris. Next year, she plans to go to Russia to learn their language. Cloie plans to work for the government as a linguist. She now can speak English and Cherokee. My dad and Cloie speak to each other all the time in Cherokee. I can pick up on some of what they are talking about, but when they start speaking fast, they lose me.

After mom, dad, and I had our showers and our robes on, we sat down on the lawn chairs. That bumpy flight took a lot out of all of us. We were very quiet and my dad dozed off and started snoring. My mom put her finger over her mouth, as if to say, be quiet. She then went into the house. When she came out, she had a tray with three glasses of ice cold lemonade. When she put it down on the table, dad opened his eyes and said, "Just what I needed." Dad has a way of taking short naps. When he wakes up, he is a brand new person.

Mom said, "The house is cooled down enough, but I think I will just grill hamburgers outside tonight. I put enough meat out to thaw for each of us to have two burgers apiece." That sounds so good for this reason – food always tastes better when it is cooked and eaten outside. Mother said she checked her emails when she went inside the house and said Cloie left a message saying she hopes we had a great vacation and missed being with us. Dad made mention that this was the first vacation that Cloie wasn't with us.

Bam was curious as to what I had in my hand, and was nudging me for some attention. Then she would stretch out her neck to smell my glass of lemonade. I let her get close enough to smell the bottom of my glass and she licked off the condensation (the liquid from the vapor the ice causes) and she looked at me like she wanted a drink from my glass. I poured some in my hand and she lapped it up. The tartness made her wiggle her tail and shake all over like she had a chill or something. We all got a chuckle out of that. I told Bam that I would be right back and went into the house to get a banana Popsicle. This is her favorite treat, a special delight that has her jumping for joy. She had her nose all over the paper and I thought she was going to take a bite out of it before I could even get the wrapper off. I have to hold on tight to the stick because I think she would even eat that because it has the banana smell embedded in it. I don't think it would digest very well though.

Mom went over to the garden to pick some vine-ripened tomatoes for our burgers. Bam followed her but stopped at least three feet from the garden because that one time of putting her nose on the solar hot wire had broken her from trying to get into the garden. Mom always throws her a couple of tomatoes, some fresh lettuce, and the tops off the onions so she's not totally deprived. Bam loves her little salad.

Dad got the fire going and I washed the tomatoes, lettuce and onions. I like to slice the tomatoes a little thick but the red onions I prefer sliced really thin. The hamburger meat and buns are thawed and ready to put on the fire. Mom puts the buns on top of the meat a couple of minutes before she takes them off the grill. Freezing bread makes it a little hard around the edges, but putting it on the burgers while they are still on the grill softens them like they were freshly made. It was so nice to have a home-cooked meal again. Two weeks of restaurant food, though fun for a time, had gotten old to all of us.

After we filled our tummies, we stretched out on the lawn chairs and talked about what we would do tomorrow. Dad talked about how high the grass was and it would probably take all day to mow it. I said the garden needed the weeds pulled and I could probably be done with it in a few hours. Mom said that the apple tree was full of apples and she thought an apple pie would be nice for dessert for tomorrow. I told her I would help pick them and maybe we could even can a few quarts for this winter. Sounds as if we have a full day planned for tomorrow.

I was still a little restless from the flight home and unable to relax, so I grabbed my basketball and started shooting some hoops. Even when just playing basketball by myself, I always have a great time. I start out close to the hoop and gradually get further and further away until I'm far enough away that if I were in a game, the basket would be a three pointer. For me, the more I practice, the better I get. The great thing about shooting hoops is you can do it all alone. It's just you and the hoop. It's a very independent feeling, to enjoy yourself getting better and better.

Basketball is my favorite sport to play because when you are on a hot streak, you can't be beaten. The more hours you put into shooting hoops, the more likely you are to get on a hot streak. In other words, the more you put into it, the more you get out of it.

My dad introduced me to basketball when I was ten years old. He put the hoop down low enough that I could make hoops with the greatest of ease. This made me feel like I was really good at this sport. I liked that feeling. As time went on, my dad would secretly raise the hoop so it became more of a challenge for me. It was a mystery to me why one day I couldn't miss and the next day I only hit one out of four hoops. By the time I was twelve years old I had figured it out. By then, he had taken it up all the way to the standard height at which games are played. When I asked him how long he had been doing this, he let me know that from the time I began shooting hoops, as soon as I mastered a height, he would raise it two inches. He told me he didn't want me to lose interest. Well, it worked, because I have a passion for shooting hoops and I'm very good at it.

On occasion, the family would take turns throwing the basketball twelve feet from the hoop. In the beginning, everyone was beating me, but now I dominate. The reason I rule by superior power over my family in basketball is that I practice constantly. That really makes a difference in your game.

My family plays basketball in our backyard for the exercise. I can tell you now that it is great exercise because you are always stretching and moving fast with the game. However, for me, it is way more than just exercise; it fulfills my competitive nature.

Dad decided to join me in shooting a few hoops. He was about twelve feet from the hoop. I stayed under the hoop to retrieve any missed hoops and try to bat them in with my hand. In a real game of basketball, it is an advantage to bat the ball back to the hoop to try and score. My dad loves to help me with this strategy. He gets a real kick out of it when I bat the ball in and make a score.

Mom was gathering the dishes to take them in the house and wash them up. I asked if she needed help and she said, "No, I've got it under control. You two have some fun."

My mom always loves to see her children have fun. It is her belief that childhood determines how stable people will be when they become adults. If you can't have fun as a child, how will you be able to have fun as an adult? This mindset has made for a great childhood for my sister, Cloie, and me.

When we were young, mom would take us to swimming lessons in the summer. It was great to be around other kids swimming and splashing around in the water. After an hour's lesson, we would stay for another hour and practice what we had learned. Cloie was four years older than me and I think she already knew how to swim but just loved watching me learn. I think she was there more as a support person than as a student. Mom joined us in the pool after the lesson was over and we would always have a great time splashing around in the water with the warm sun beating down on our bodies. These are some of my fondest memories of when I was really young. After we had finished swimming, we would go to the swings. I loved to move rhythmically back and forth suspended in the air. It was like flying. The swing was a very large set and we covered a lot of distance when moving back and forth. Sometimes, I would lean back with my arms straight out and watch the clouds move as I swung. It felt like I was in the clouds.

My mom always says that children can have fun without breaking the bank. Children love for their parents to play with them, all the way up to when they leave home and become semi-adults. My parents practice the holistic approach to raising children. They emphasize the importance of having a healthy relationship with their children as people and having fun is a big part of that. Interaction in a positive and fun relationship creates a stable environment where children can flourish.

Mom also says that we live at a cellular level and we are what we eat. This is why we always have five fruits and five vegetables every day. She believes the reason inherited chronic diseases exist is because of our ancestors' bad diets. We inherited their starving cells. If you give it much thought, it does make a lot of sense.

We have a honey bee hive and use honey as a sweetener instead of sugar. When mom makes tea, she pours the honey into the hot water with the tea bags. Heating it helps it mix in. We grow a lot of different herbs and make our own tea bags with pieces of cheesecloth. My favorite is sage. It makes my skin glow. I'm so lucky to have a family that cares enough to provide for me the knowledge to care for my mind and body so life can be good.

My dad tends the beehives and, although it's his favorite hobby, when he collects the honey from the hive, it makes my skin crawl. The bees, to begin with, are all over the wooden fence and the box they live in. My dad just walks right up to them and pulls out the rack with the honey, and scrapes off the honey into a bowl. The bees are landing on him and buzzing all over in the air. He just lets them crawl all over his body like they are not even there. I don't know how he does it. Dad calls them his little friends who work hard all day to feed him. I see them as hairy-bodied stinging insects that suck nectar and gather pollen from the flowers, which I appreciate – from a distance. Dad does wear a net over his face to keep the bees out of his eyes. He says he needs to see to get the honey out. If I ever retrieve honey, it will take the whole bee suit, from head to toe.

My parents believe in staying as close to nature as possible when it comes to our diet. Processed foods have a lot of the nutrition processed out of them. They believe the closer you stay to nature the longer and more productive life you will live. After all, it's not how long you live, it's how good you feel while you are alive that is important.

The next morning I gathered apples for mom to make the apple pie. She first peels and cuts the apples; then she puts them in the pie dish and covers them with ground cinnamon, honey, and pineapple juice. No crust on the bottom, just the top. For the crust, she uses wheat flour combined with olive oil and water. She pokes holes into the layer of crust and then spreads pads of butter across the top of the pie. After that, she drizzles honey across the top of the pie to sweeten the crust. Everything put into this pie has nutritional value and it tastes great.

I always like to watch mom put the pie together; she really enjoys tapping into her creative ability to make tasty dishes that feed our cells. She calls it her artistic persona – the role she assumes in order to display her conscious intentions to keep the family healthy.

After the pie hit the oven, I took the peelings out to Bam. She ate them up like she was starving. That is not the case, because just fifty feet away is the apple tree with apples all over the ground. I think Bam just likes to be fed from my hand. After Bam finished eating all the apple peelings, I grabbed a bucket and headed for the apple tree to gather apples for canning. We keep a long stick with a claw on the end to reach the apples that are up too high to reach by hand. This is a great tool and a lot of fun for picking apples. There is no apple that can escape me with this claw tool.

After my bucket was filled, I put it in a wagon to pull to the house. Bam was in a playful mood and was running circles around me and the wagon. It was a sight to see. Dad was mowing the lawn and having to empty the grass catcher after every strip he mowed. We have a mulch bin that we put leaves, grass and rotten apples in, which we use in the garden soil every year. After I unloaded the apples for mom to can, I went back to the tree to gather rotten apples for the mulch bin. I wear gloves for this job because it can be pretty nasty. The red wasps are all over these rotten apples, but they don't bother me. However, the yellow wasps can have their apples because they have stung me in the past and I avoid them at all costs. Bam was keeping me company when suddenly she jumped straight up into the air. This got my attention. I could feel something was not right when out of the bushes came a wild hog with tusks (elongated pointed teeth extending outside the hog's mouth). It came charging at my wagon and turned it over. I screamed and it turned and ran back into the bushes. I ran to my dad and told him what had happened. He told me to go in the house and get his rifle. I was running toward the house and suddenly my legs just went out from under me. I was so frightened that I was losing control of my legs; they were trembling, as was my whole body. I managed to get up but found myself falling again after only a few steps. Bam started nudging me with her nose. It was as if she were trying to help me up. I started crying uncontrollably. I was crawling toward the back door of the house when my Mother walked out the door. She ran over and asked me what was wrong. I told her a wild boar hog attacked my wagon and that dad needed his rifle. She helped me to my feet and we went into the house. Mom pulled out a chair at the kitchen table and told me to stay seated until she got back. She grabbed dad's rifle and some bullets and out the door she went.

Through the window, I watched her give dad his rifle. I couldn't stand just yet and my body was still shaking all over. Dad disappeared into the woods and mom came back toward the house. I could feel myself finally begin gaining control of my body. I dried the tears from my eyes as mom walked into the house. She came over to me, grabbed my hand and said, "What happened?" I got up from my chair and we walked to the sliding glass doors to watch for my dad's return. I began to tell her about the wild boar hog attacking my wagon. "First, there was an awful smell and Bam jumped straight up in the air and started running toward the house. A very eerie feeling came over me and then out of the bushes a wild boar hog came charging at me. If the wagon had not been between us, he likely would have killed me. He looked to weigh around 120 pounds and the tusks coming out of his mouth were probably five inches long. He looked me right in the eye and started charging. The closer he got, the stronger the foul smell. Mom, I believe if he had not caught his tusk on the side of the wagon he would have killed me!"

After listening to my story, mom called the wildlife refuge to report the incident. Though she didn't say so, I could tell she was getting really worried about dad's safety. When she hung up the phone she told me they were sending two officers to come to the house to investigate the incident.

When the officers arrived, my Mother instructed me to stay in the house. She escorted the officers to the apple tree where the boar had rammed the wagon. It was a metal wagon and was bent to the point I was sure it would never roll again. The officers looked at each other and one said, "We have a real problem here. This animal could do some real damage to a person if he managed to do all this to a steel wagon. Ma'am, this officer will escort you back to your house; we need to hunt this boar down and destroy him."

When my mom came back into the house, she grabbed me and said, "Oh, Chelsea, you must have been so frightened. That awful beast could have killed you. What he did to that wagon made the hair on the back of my head stand up. It could have been you. I think we need a cup of chamomile herbal tea."

Chamomile tea has a way of calming and creating an inner peaceful and tranquil state of mind and I was hoping it would have that effect on me now. I can't recall ever being this frightened. Not even the plane ride home from Washington compares to this experience. It could be because I was all alone, except for Bam, and she left me when she saw the wild boar hog. I don't think I will ever forget the sound of the boar hitting the wagon with his tusk. I just thank God that the wagon was between us.

Just then, a shot rang out from deep in the woods; then another and another - three shots in less than a minute. I hope this is the end of that nightmarish wild boar hog. This has been an intensely distressing experience and if the boar is not killed, I will have problems being outside by myself from now on. I will always be looking at the bushes around me thinking he will be lurking behind one of them, ready to put a tusk through my body.

Even the chamomile tea can't calm me down. There is just too much adrenalin running in my veins. In school, we studied the medulla oblongata, which is the nerve tissue at the base of the brain that controls respiration, circulation, and various other bodily functions, including the secretion of the hormone called epinephrine. I think this is what happened to me today. Epinephrine is what a person is given to start the heart when it stops beating. Well, my heart feels like it is still beating way too fast.

My mom walked over to the window and said, "Chelsea, come here and take a look at this." When I got to the window, I saw the two officers and my dad walking toward the house. The two officers were holding the back legs of that awful wild boar hog, dragging him toward the house. They were having a high old time laughing and talking to each other. Mom said, "Let's go see what they have." We walked out to meet them and sure enough, it was that stinking old boar hog that ruined my wagon. Dad said, "Hey, Chelsea, do you recognize this thing?" I replied, "Yes, that's him." Dad said, "You won't have to worry about him anymore. I'm going to have his head sent to a taxidermist to be filled with stuffing and then I'll mount him in the barn. This is the largest wild boar hog any of us have ever seen. He must weigh at least 140 pounds. These tusks are unbelievable as well as the biggest any of us have ever seen. Look here, Chelsea, there is red paint from the wagon on his tusk."

Seeing this beast dead was the only thing that had been able to calm me down. It was closure. Knowing he would never be able to jump out of a bush and get me allowed my composure to begin coming back and I noticed a tranquility of mind returning as well. I gave my dad a hug and said, "Thank you, dad. Is that the ugliest, most repulsive, hideous creature you've ever seen? Are you sure you want him in the barn?" Dad said, "I want to be able to show people the most offensive, unattractive, and displeasing to the eye creature ever to walk on this earth." We all started laughing.

What are the odds of having two near-death experiences in just one week? I would say they are pretty long odds. After a day like today, I'm going to have a long talk with God before I go to sleep. I'm going to thank Him for not taking me to heaven just yet. I have eternity to spend in Heaven, but only a hundred or so years here on earth. Everybody has their own idea as to what heaven will be like, but I personally think there are levels. Just like on earth, you have people who live very hard lives and people who live charmed lives. Both have equal opportunity at a chance to go to heaven. Jesus said in John 14:2, "In my Father's house there are many dwelling places; otherwise, how could I have told you that I was going to prepare a place for you?" I have a lot of good things left to do on earth and I think God has plans for me here and this is why he protected me this week. I hope I can be worthy of God's plans for me.

I believe that God prepares dwellings of different levels. One spirit may have a house while another will have a mansion in heaven. It all depends on how closely you live up to God's word, the Bible. My goal is to live in a mansion for eternity and all I have to do is to live my life according to the Gospels of the New Testament. It may be the whole chapter or only a couple of verses each day, but I visit the Bible every day.

The next morning I woke up before my mom or dad and decided to fix breakfast for them. Because we had been gone for two weeks, everything for breakfast had to come from the freezer. I started with link sausage because they're small enough to thaw fast. Wheat bread and frozen orange juice work well also. We scrambled eggs and froze them uncooked before we left on vacation to be sure they would still be good when we got home from our trip.

Mom and dad like to stay up late when they are off work, so they stay in bed a little later in the mornings than they do on work days. Their three-week vacation is almost over and I always try to make things easier for them during their last week of vacation – they deserve it. They work hard all year long, and besides, I get three months off for the summer.

While everything was thawing, I went to the backyard, grabbed a chair and sat down to watch the sun come up. That is my favorite part of the day. What I like most about the early morning is all the moisture in the air. It makes the air smell so good. We have morning glory flowers that are open in the early part of the day; they are as blue as the sky on a clear day. Dad put chicken wire around the poles that sport these beautiful vines so they would flourish. They climb all the way to the top of the pole, and then grow another two feet, as if reaching for the sky. They take my breath away with their beauty.

As I stretched out on a lawn chair, I saw Bam coming out of the woods. She spotted me and was running to greet me. The first thing she does is check my hands to see if I have a treat. I always grab a couple of jelly beans, just in case she comes around; I hold my hands out with the jelly beans in one or the other to see if she can guess which hand they are in. She always picks the right hand – the one that's holding the jelly beans; I think she can smell them.

The first thing I said to her was, "That sure was a close one yesterday. Thank you for warning me." She probably doesn't even remember, but I'm grateful anyway. I scratched her behind her ear and she was in heaven.

Two years ago, a young girl fell down in a pen full of hogs and they ate her; yes, hogs will eat humans. It was an awful tragedy. All that was left of her was her clothes, shoes and some hair. The whole town was devastated. I thanked God again for not letting me be killed by that hog yesterday. I gave Bam another hug and said, "Thanks again for the warning."

It was time to go back inside to fix breakfast for my mom and dad so I could surprise them with breakfast in bed before they get up. I knocked on their bedroom door and asked if they were decent. Their reply was to give them five minutes. I went back to the kitchen and loaded up the tray with their breakfast and headed back to their room. I knocked on the door again and this time they asked me to come in. When I opened the door and they saw the food, mom said, "Chelsea, you are so sweet." Dad said, "That's my girl." I put the tray on the nightstand next to the bed and handed them their plates. I sat in the chair at the foot of the bed and drank my orange juice while they ate.

After we chatted awhile and finished breakfast, I said to them, "You know, you guys are lucky because that hog could have killed me and eaten me like that poor girl a couple of years ago. You wouldn't have anybody to fix you breakfast." Mom said, "Sweetheart, when I saw that wagon, I thought about that poor girl myself. We are so lucky you didn't get hurt." Dad said, "Come here and give me a hug." With that I laid the hog to rest.

As the week ended and my parents went back to work, I started doing my chores for money, and was once again saving for next summer's vacation. Even though I had laid the memory of the hog to rest, sometimes I still remembered anyway, but I refused to think about that wild hog. Every time I put money in my piggy bank I was reminded I have a future and so if the thought of him tried to creep into my mind, I shut him out. That's what you have to do with bad thoughts – just shut them out.

As the summer was ending, thoughts of my friends

came across my mind. School will be starting again soon. I have a birthday next week and I will turn 15 years old. This is a milestone, a significant event in the history of my life. Because my parents promised me freedom to make decisions about my life and because I will be spending more time with friends than at any time in my life, I asked for God's guidance in my decision making.

Chapter 2
Friends

Every summer I have mixed emotions about vacation. I love my family, but I have such good times with my friends and will not see them until the following school year. I just miss them in the summertime. I even miss the kids who are not my friends.

My school just happens to have a lot of fancifully eccentric students. There's this one kid called Jake who has exceptional intellectual and creative abilities; in other words, he is a freaking genius. He is truly a one of a kind in a school of just normal everyday students. Once we had this science project on solar energy. Jake brought a toy car on which he had put a solar panel on the roof with a fan attached to the back. Somehow the solar panel made the fan turn, which made the car move. I look for this type of technology to be used in the future.

Jake has good manners and is always polite but keeps others at a distance. No one can get close to him. I think his mind is stuck in high gear. During lunch hour he sits by himself and reads or works on algebra problems. Once I asked him what he was up to and his answer was, "Solving an expression in which only numbers and arithmetic operations are contained or used." What kind of kid talks like that? Talk about intimidation. I felt he was trying to discourage me from talking to him; instead it became a challenge for me to get to know him. Most of the kids at school buddy up with someone who is equal or less than they perceive themselves to be. I personally looked for comrades whom I felt were above me mentally or even physically. It made life more exciting. Jake has a quality that holds my attention; in intelligence, he has superior mental power. He is rational rather than emotional. This makes us opposites, directly contrary in nature. Once I stopped Jake at his locker and asked him if he would help me with my algebra. He agreed to come to my house but insisted my parents be present. I thought that was so cute because my parents would not have left us alone anyway. He didn't need to know that; it was my secret. Normally, it is the girl wanting protection, but Jake is anything but normal or typical. We had a platonic relationship, transcending physical desire and tending toward friendship. I made an A in algebra and made a friend for life. Jake made it clear his friendship would always be there for me.

Another friend, BreAnna, is an ace basketball player who is my best friend. She is 5 feet 9 inches tall and drop-dead gorgeous. She has many attractive features: great hair, sharp features, slender body and most impressive, her height. She hopes to be a model and coach when she graduates from high school. Hanging out with BreAnna always makes for an exciting day. People just notice her; she stands out. This brings all her friends attention by proxy just because they happen to be with her. This is okay with me, for I have had the chance to meet many people through my friendship with BreAnna. She is also intelligent and a lot of fun to be with.

We became friends on the basketball court. I was great about getting the ball down the court, and BreAnna encouraged me to pass the ball to her, and she would make a lay-up for an easy score. Our fans surely envision our savvy and protection of points on the board to add up to a winning season. We shared the glory of each hoop scored. This year, the competition was stiff but with my quickness and BreAnna's height under the basket, we had a winning season. We played off each other's strengths. I only missed one game and it was the only game we lost the whole season. This lets me know how important my presence is. It is a good feeling.

BreAnna is extremely self-conscious and, consequently, shy because she is so much taller than everyone else. When she looks at herself in the mirror, all she sees is an average-looking girl. BreAnna just can't see what everybody else sees. Fellow students are unable to tell the difference between her shyness and being stuck up, hence she acquired the label of being a snob. Most thought she was stuck on herself. Nothing could be further from the truth.

Toward the end of the basketball season comes the playoff games. Well, this means the team gets to load up on the bus and travel to another state. This puts the team at a higher energy level than any experienced throughout the season. The vibe pulsing through the team is a rhythmical beating of one.

After everyone was loaded onto the bus we hit the highway and headed for Big D, you know, Dallas. We sang songs and talked about how badly we were going to beat our opponent in the battle for Number One.

Upon our arrival at our hotel, we paired off and checked into our rooms. After freshening up, we met for dinner and discussed our game plan for victory over our opposing force. During the dinner in the restaurant there were some mighty fine-looking young men who were checking out BreAnna, as usual. After dinner, while heading for our rooms, one of them asked BreAnna if she and her friend would like to hang out - her friend being yours truly, me. BreAnna said we had a couple of hours, and just what did they have in mind. First, they introduced themselves as Charles and Jonathan and then suggested we take a ride in an elevator that would take us to the highest point in Dallas. "It is quite a sight to see. The lights in this town will take your breath away," Jonathan said. So off we went; it felt like we are going straight to heaven. Higher and higher until I started feeling dizzy – a sort of whirling sensation. Finally, the elevator came to a stop. When I looked down I had a sense of falling, as if the gravity were pulling me down. Jonathan held my hand and asked if I was alright. I told him I've always had a problem dealing with heights. He said to just hold on to his hand and everything would be fine. After awhile, the sensations lessened. I was then able to enjoy the most spectacular sight my eyes had ever seen. The lights were twinkling as far as the eye could see. My heart was full of happiness. We were having a great time; nothing serious, just good clean fun and that made it ever better.

BreAnna and Charles seemed to be having a good time as well. BreAnna is normally really quiet around guys, but knowing she would probably never see Charles again somehow made her braver and, consequently, more open. All of a sudden, Charles gave BreAnna a quick kiss, but then he began apologizing immediately, saying he just couldn't help himself because she was so beautiful. BreAnna immediately closed back up and told Charles there was no justification for what he had done and to please take her back to her hotel room. Charles looked so embarrassed and frustrated as he and Jonathan walked us back to the floor where our room was. BreAnna had to have seen the look on his face when we got to our door because she explained to Charles that she must stay focused on her playoff basketball game in the morning. She told him it had been an exciting evening and thanked him for showing her Dallas from way up high. Before we closed the door, I asked, "Just how old are you guys anyway?" "Seventeen," Jonathan replied. I nodded, and then shut the door.

Morning came rushing through the windows with a

shower of sunshine. Excitement from the previous night still hung in the air, but it was time to focus on the championship game. The team met downstairs for a light breakfast, then off to the arena to change into our team uniforms. Our eagerness to get on the court is palpable and, believe me, all the hard work to get here is worth it.

The stadium was filling up with spectators representing each team; I've never been in a stadium this large and I began to feel a little overwhelmed deep in my soul. I had no idea so many people would be watching our game. After we filed into the stadium, Coach Sims gave a motivating talk. She said, "You have earned the right to compete for this championship game and make your family and yourselves proud of the win you are about to make. As for me, I'm already proud of each one of you for getting to this arena. This is my piece of cake, and when you win, it will be the icing on my piece of cake. Now, get out there and warm up for ten minutes; then let's go win this game!"

We, the Pink Ravens, hit the floor looking good in our pink and white uniforms. Each team member ran down the floor, made a basket; the next team player would catch the ball, pass it and start all over. We were in sync and able to feed off each other's energy. This is a recipe for a win.

Our opponents were warming up on the opposite end of the court. I looked them over and said to myself that we can get these girls. They'd better look out for the Pink Ravens because here we come.

Although the Blue Jays looked to be faster than our girls, they didn't have the same level of coordination. When they were passing the ball, they dropped it often. I don't know if this will continue after they are through warming up, but if it does, they are toast.

The referee blew the whistle for the start of the game, and Coach Sims chose BreAnna to start the game by jumping against the opponent. BreAnna tipped the ball right in my direction; I caught it and down the floor toward the basket I went. I put the ball in the air and two points were on the board – just like that. By halftime, we were ahead by six points. Coach Sims let us know she wanted chocolate icing with sprinkles on top of her cake. We all got a kick out of her sense of humor. We were on fire and having the time of our lives.

The second half of the game seemed to be picking up on the exceptionally great concentration of power by our opponent. The Blue Jays were bumping into us and taking the foul. They were using teammates who were not starters and important to their game just to foul us. You don't want your best players to get fouled out. It was as if they sent out the thugs to rough us up. What was happening was brutal.

They doubled up on BreAnna and fouled her twofold. None of us were sure how much abuse BreAnna would be able to take. This team was aware that half of the points on the board were because of BreAnna under the basket, but they also knew she was not good at the free throw line.

Their strategy was to put BreAnna out of the game and it was working. We still had the lead but now it was only a two point lead. This was giving the Blue Jays a boost. They became even more aggressive and doubled up on BreAnna with their largest players. This time, BreAnna fell to the floor with a loud thud that sounded like she broke every bone in her body. The medics rushed out on the floor to attend to her injury. She was not moving and we were not sure if she was even alive. They brought out the stretcher and six men loaded her on it without bending her body. They rushed her out to the locker room. Our hearts dropped to our feet.

Coach Sims told us to be strong and take those Blue Jays down with a win. She then left the floor to be with BreAnna. When Coach Sims entered the locker room, she saw BreAnna had her eyes open. The medic would not allow her to sit up yet. He was checking her eyes with a flashlight.

Coach Sims demanded, "What's her condition?" The medic responded, "She just had the wind knocked out of her and wants to finish the game. We will see how she does in the next five minutes." Coach Sims said, "I will be back in five minutes."

Coach Sims returned to the floor and told the team that BreAnna was awake and asking to play out the rest of the game. This was an inspiration to all the Pink Raven girls and we hit the floor with a vengeance. It was as if just the thought of retribution put energy in every one of us. It was truly amazing how the degree of accuracy increased with our knowledge of BreAnna's recovery.

The points were adding up on the scoreboard for the Pink Ravens as they had been when BreAnna was in the game. The team was coming on point like we'd never experienced before and we began regaining our lead, this time by ten points.

Coach Sims returned to the locker room to check on BreAnna's status. Her heart filled with joy when she saw BreAnna sitting in an upright position. They locked eyes on one another and BreAnna said, "Coach, I'm ready to play." Coach Sims looked at the medic and he shook his head indicating this was not a good idea. Coach Sims said to BreAnna, "Honey, we need you on the side lines to inspire the team, but I can't risk your health right now." BreAnna reluctantly agreed, but only because when she stood up on her shaky legs, she realized she was more shaken up than she'd thought.

When BreAnna entered the stadium, the entire audience stood up and cheered. Even the fans who came to cheer on the Blue Jays were cheering for BreAnna's recovery. People, as a whole, don't approve of athletes doubling up to hurt another player. Everyone clearly hoped for her recovery.

The Pink Ravens proved to have a stronger endurance and will to win the game. I made a three-point basket, which gave me an incredible high. This basket was the last made, which gave us a thirteen-point lead. The final score was 73 to 60. Our team was super-excited and ready to celebrate our victory with a ceremony in honor of Coach Sims. The festive celebration was capped off with a cake with chocolate icing covered with sprinkles!

The next morning when the team gathered for breakfast, just guess who was there. You guessed it – Charles and Jonathan! They were doing everything in their power to get our attention, but this breakfast belongs to the team, so we did our best to ignore them.

After breakfast, we had one hour before loading onto the bus to go home. When BreAnna and I got up from the table, Charles and Jonathan were immediately right on our heels. Charles said, "You girls were great yesterday. BreAnna, I'm so glad you are all right. I was so worried when I saw you lying on the court." BreAnna said, "That's so sweet of you to be concerned about my welfare." Jonathan said to me, "That three-point basket you made at the end of the game was amazing, Chelsea." I said, "Thank you, Jonathan. I'm glad you guys got to see the game." They clearly wanted to hang out for awhile, but we still had to pack and make sure we didn't miss our ride home. We talked for a few more minutes, let them know what a good time we'd had with them and that we hoped to see them again next year at the playoffs. Then we set off for our room to finish packing.

The team loaded onto the bus and we headed out for home. We were still on a high and filled with joy after winning the game. We talked about how we stripped the ball right out of the Blue Jay's hands and made a score, and how the Blue Jays were in violation of the rules when they attacked BreAnna. Most of all, we chanted the final score. The sense of oneness and of victory left a sweet taste none of us had ever experienced before. Although I know that what goes up must come down, I couldn't help but think it would be great if this feeling could last forever. I kept thinking that some really lucky people were professional basketball players who actually get paid to feel sweet victory. Now that sounds like the perfect job to me – getting paid to do what you love, signing autographs, taking pictures; yes, that sounds like the good life to me.

You know, there are things like scholarships and financial aid awarded to students who excel at sports; that just might be my ticket to my future. If our team continues to win, we will be noticed and, just maybe, we'll get our college paid for. How cool that would be to get to play basketball, have college paid for, live in the dorm and do all those fun college things just because I'm good at playing basketball. I bet my parents would also love it because college is very expensive these days. I think this will be a goal I will strive for.

Coach Sims asked if anyone was hungry and should we stop for lunch and, in complete harmony, we all replied, "Yes!" We were all famished – starved to death. The bus pulled into a parking lot of a very large mall. Coach Sims told us after lunch we were free to explore the mall but we had to be back on the bus in two hours. Although we were still on a high, this put the team back up at an even higher energy level; everyone knows there's just something about a mall and teenagers – they just go together.

BreAnna and I grabbed a quick burger and drink and were off to explore the mall. Our money was low, but window shopping is still a blast even if you can't afford to buy anything. Also, boy watching is one of our favorite pastimes, and the mall was loaded.

Texas seems to do things in a larger way than what I have ever seen. We could put three of our malls in just this one. I love the way they set up their display windows; you know immediately what style each store carries. What I noticed was the abundant amount of leather these shops carry. It must be because they have all these cattle ranches raising our food, but thank God, they don't waste the skins. I just love the smell of leather. Leather keeps you warm in the winter without burning you up like synthetic chemical compound materials can. I'm also into natural cotton, as in jeans. Texas has a lot of both and I'm in shopping heaven.

We came across an accessory shop full of nonessential but useful decorative handbags, belts and hairclips. I saw an oversized handbag in pink leather and told BreAnna I just had to go in and touch that bag. I asked the clerk in the store if she would get the pink bag in the display window so I could look at it. She said she had one in the back and she would go get it. While she was gone, I noticed a pink leather belt that was a perfect match. "Only $7.00; what a buy! The clerk was returning with the oversize bag and I asked BreAnna to hold the belt while I rummaged through the bag thoroughly searching out each compartment of storage. At one time, I put my entire head into this bag, and took a deep breath of the wonderful smell of leather. When I finished, I looked up and said, "Thank you God for this cow." I looked at BreAnna and the clerk and they were chuckling with amusement of my admiration of this cow's skin. I asked the clerk how much the purse cost. The clerk said, "This is your lucky day; the purse's original price was $90.00 but the sales price is $40.00. I looked at BreAnna and said, "All I have is $30.00." BreAnna said, "What a pity; I can see how much you love the purse." I sighed and said, "You're right. You know, mom and dad gave me a Visa card for emergencies and though it will cost me my allowance for a few weeks; I do love the purse enough that I'm going to go ahead and use my emergency card to make up the difference between the cost and what money I have." This truly was my lucky day. The clerk bagged up my purchase, handed it to me and said, "Ya'll come see us again." I was so excited about my purchase that on my way out of the store I clasped my hands together and said, "Yes," rather loudly.

Time was running out and we would not be able to see the whole mall. We decided to take the glass elevator to the top where we could get a good view; it was awesome to look at how huge this mall was. We looked at each other and said, "Wow!" I told BreAnna, "When we are old enough to drive a car, we gotta come back to this place." She said, "Absolutely!"

On the way back down in the glass elevator, we noticed a couple of guys staring at us. By the time we got to the bottom floor they were waiting at the elevator door. As we stepped off, one of them asked, "Did you have a good ride?" I replied, "It was perfect." They offered to show us around the mall, but we explained time was a factor and we were actually on our way to a bus that would be taking us home. They just kind of followed our footsteps and talked about themselves, obviously trying to impress us. In our brief walk to the bus, we got to hear about how they lived on a ranch and worked with horses. They talked about how they brought horses from wildness into a domesticated state. In other words, they tamed them. Wow! That sounded exciting. They talked about how some day they would like to enter competition in the national rodeo circuit as bronco-riding and steer-wrestling cowboys. It sounded dangerous to me; I've been horseback riding before, but the tame horses always scare me.

We got back to the bus with about ten minutes to spare. These two guys never even asked us our names or told us theirs. We continued to let them talk about themselves without knowing who they were; we figured we would never see them again anyway, so we just listened to whatever stories they had to tell. My favorite story was the one about when they were branding a calf. They told how it was roped, then taken to the ground and a hot iron put to its side to let the world know who owns it. After the hot iron was pulled back, the rope was removed and the calf was set free. Well, this particular little calf did not like this at all and started charging the guys. Because this is such an unusual behavior, the guys were not on their guard and the calf headed for their buttocks with full force. The calf headed between them and caught one cheek of each guy's buttock. They both went down and the calf looked back at them like, "Now we're even!" We all got a good laugh out of this story and then said our goodbyes. Everyone loaded up on the bus and off we went.

We kicked around reasons why these two guys never told us their names or asked us ours. Were they afraid, did they not think to ask, or was it they were just looking for a little detached conversation? Whatever the case, we had a good time.

Coach Sims thanked us for being back on time and said we were just a great, responsible bunch of kids that she enjoyed sharing time with. Then she asked us to share stories about what we did with the two hours in the huge mall. I raised my hand to be the first to share my shopping experience. I passed my new pink purse around the bus and recommended everyone put their head inside and smell the great leather aroma. I told them the purse would be my victory reminder of when the Pink Ravens hammered the Blue Jays. Everyone in the bus stood up and cheered. Another team member had a coffee cup engraved with "Pink Ravens beat the Blue Jays" and everyone stood up again and chanted "Pink Ravens, Pink Ravens." Coach Sims next revealed what she had purchased and the real reason for our two-hour lunch break – she lifted a large bag out of a seat and pulled out a handful of white tee shirts with pink print that said Pink Ravens. She began throwing these tees to each team member and said, "This is my way of saying, 'Thank you'." Everyone on the bus was full of unrestrained enthusiasm and overflowing joy while we shouted back, "Thank you, Coach Sims."

Chapter 3
Their Gain, My Loss

You remember my friends Jake, the genius, and BreAnna, the basketball player? Well, just what do you think happened when they were introduced to each other? Sparks were flying! Yes, they were perfect for each other.

I have no one to blame but myself for this feeling of loss. I thought going to the movie with my best friends would be a lot of fun. Well, it was ... for them. They became so engrossed with one another that I became invisible. Oh, it hurts so much! You know the old saying, "Two's company, three's a crowd." Jake and BreAnna were trying very hard to include me, but when two people click as they did and it's a brand new feeling, they just can't help themselves. Well, anyway, they make a great couple.

After the movie, we went to the ice cream shop next door. This is when things were really getting out of hand. They were laughing and talking as if I weren't even there. I don't think BreAnna understood half of what Jake was saying, but she was still hanging on to every word he said. It was so obvious she didn't understand him, but he loved her look of attentiveness. Jake was oblivious to the fact that BreAnna was my best friend and he was capturing her heart. I so wanted to be happy for them, but at this time, my heart is broken. Best friends don't come around that often in life, so I will just have to accept their relationship and be the third party. That is, if they'll let me.

Jake's parents were picking us up in fifteen minutes and I was so ready for this night to be over. I have never had to deal with the feeling of being left out of the loop before. I hope I'm never guilty of making a human being feel like I'm feeling now.

Jake bought me a cup of Rocky Road chocolate ice cream and BreAnna had Vanilla Pecan. Jake had plain vanilla with fudge topping. Ice cream has a way of bringing happiness into the air so the mood was changing into a more friendly and inclusive atmosphere. We started having a three-way conversation about how good the ice cream was and how much fun it was to go to a movie together. It was like they were back to themselves, but just when I was starting to have fun again, Jake's parents showed up. They knew their son was not the typical teenage boy and so they were happy to see him enjoying himself with friends. This scenario made for one of the best days in Jake's life, but one of the worst for me. I'm sure being a teenager makes things way too dramatic. Mom and dad always tell me things are just a bigger deal to a teenager.

BreAnna asked if she could spend the night and I said sure. She popped open her cell phone and was immediately begging her mom for permission to stay the night. Her mom didn't have a problem with it, so off we went to my house. BreAnna could not talk about anything but Jake. She talked about how dreamy he was and why didn't we get together a long time ago. Next thing I knew she was on the phone talking to Jake. They had obviously planned the whole thing; BreAnna's mother would never let her talk to a boy on the phone all night. Once again, I got put on the backburner and now Jake is no longer a nerd; he has joined the real world of being cool. I feel so used. I'm trying to understand by putting myself in BreAnna's place. But I just don't think I would exclude a friend like she was excluding me.

I guess I fell asleep while they were talking. I woke

up at 9:00 a.m. while BreAnna slept till noon. When she finally woke up, she said she needed to go home. She had a date with Jake at 3:00 and needed to go shopping for a new outfit, take a shower, and do her nails and hair. I could feel her excitement and just couldn't help feeling jealous; after all, Jake was my friend first. She did not invite me to go with them. This is when I realized I needed to find a new friend or just be without companionship for the rest of my life. I'm sure, when the new wears off, they will have time for me again, but I can't wait that long. It could be months before that happens.

Monday morning during first hour English, BreAnna slipped me a note. When I opened it she wrote all about the date she had with Jake. Although I was happy BreAnna and Jake had a good time, I had other emotions as well and I was afraid my deep sense of loss might have the tears start falling on my paper. To avoid having anyone know my hurt, I keep my head down so no one can see my teary eyes – from my weeping heart. BreAnna wrote about how Jake held her hand the whole time they were together on this super date. She made such an impression on his parents that they invited her to their house next weekend for another date. There was no mention of me hanging out with them on this date either. I guess I'm history.

My fourth hour is math, and guess who is in this class? Yep, Jake. He's not much for passing notes, but rather whispers when the teacher works math problems on the chalkboard. He whispered, "That BreAnna is really hot." Oh, my gosh. Jake is talking like a regular kid and all I could say was, "I'm glad you like her." I felt like such a liar. Then Jake said, "I like everything about her." I thought, a little bitterly, there was a time when I felt that way too. Now I was thinking of her as a user and someone who has stolen my best friend. I thought fourth hour would never end.

After fourth hour comes lunch and, in the past, I've

always shared it with BreAnna. Since I wasn't at all sure what would happen, thoughts of skipping lunch entered my mind, but my stomach was assuring me I would never make it to sixth hour without food. I knew I would have to face the music and so I headed for the cafeteria. By the time I got there, Jake and BreAnna were already at a table together. I so longed for the day when Jake sat by himself doing math problems and BreAnna and I shared lunch and great stories – alone.

By the time I got my tray and sat down, Jake and BreAnna were so engrossed in their conversation they didn't even notice me at all. Invisible again, I thought. It was at least five minutes before they even acknowledged I was there; they gave me a smile and went right back to talking to each other. This let me know I will have to find a new life; not today, because I'm just too sad, but by tomorrow anyway.

The day was finally over and I was in my room, with the door closed. My heart was full of sadness, my throat filled with a lump and finally the tears just could not be contained. I started crying and knew I was no longer in control of my body. My chest was heaving and I was sobbing loudly. Thank goodness, my parents weren't home yet because I really didn't want to have to explain what was wrong with me. I must have cried for at least twenty minutes; this hasn't happened to me in years. I don't know why, but crying always seems to make me feel better. It's like taking a bath; you just feel cleaner and fresher.

The next day, I woke up late and missed my first hour class. This has never happened to me before. I must be depressed. I have always had the ability to rebound from bad situations. I have to quit feeling sorry for myself and put together a game plan to find my own happiness. It's inside me; I know this – I just need to find it. My plan is to break out of my comfort zone and look for new friends.

Second hour class with Mrs. Smith is debate and government; you know, the study of the process of governing and the control of public policy in a political unit. Isn't that a mouthful? Political science is not my favorite subject and on top of that I was having one of the worst weeks of my life. I decided it was time for me to take control of the situation and turn around my dislike for political science (plus my depression from losing my best friends) with something positive. I decided I was going to take an interest in how my government works and find a new friend who likes political science to make it more exciting. Hopefully, that would take my mind off everything else.

As I looked around the classroom, I saw many interesting faces. I was pleased to note that as I took an interest in the other students, they seemed to take on a whole new persona (that's the role a person assumes in order to display his or her conscious intentions). As I listened to the class discussion, each student seemed to have his or her own idea of what our government should or should not have control over. Mrs. Smith always encourages her students to debate these ideas. In debate, every student's goal is to change the minds of the other students to see things their way. Most of what has influenced each student has come from the values within their own family. Our textbook had defined family as something like, "A fundamental social group in society consisting of a man and woman and their offspring," and continued to clarify by the concept of, "who think somewhat alike." I think that's a pretty good description, although I think it also includes people sharing a common ancestry. This would mean your grandparents, and their parents and so on and on.

One of the students, Zack, always wanted to discuss gun control. The reason he is so passionate about this subject is that his family has a tradition of bird and deer hunting. His father and grandfather are hunters and he wants to be able to carry on his family tradition. He fears, and probably rightly, that if certain laws were to be passed against guns, the government would have to enforce these laws and a family tradition would be lost.

Other issues that came up during that debate were the right to defend your family and the right to bear arms. In other words, if the bad guy has a gun, you need equal protection from him – the right to have your own gun. Zack has his own idea on this subject; take all the guns away from the bad guys so only the good guys have guns. Sounds like a good solution to me. I admire Zack's passion and think he would make a good employee for the government someday.

Another student named Sara was concerned about the power people with a cause can get through lobbyists. Lobbyists are people who try to influence legislators to pass laws in favor of their particular interests. Sara is afraid if someone doesn't stop these people, she may never get to eat another chicken leg. Sara even quotes the Bible - Genesis, chapter 1, verse 26: "Then God said: 'Let us make man in our image, after our likeness. Let them have dominion over the fish of the sea, the birds of the air, and the cattle, and over all the wild animals and all the creatures that crawl on the ground.'" Sara said that God gave us control over all creatures and this right should not be taken away. She continued, "Because someone thinks people should only eat vegetables, they can try to get a law passed where eating animals is a crime. In my opinion, that's bizarre! We need to make it against the law for anyone to lobby away our rights."

"You go, Sara," I thought to myself. Sara had such passion she got me to thinking, "What if I weren't allowed to ever eat another chicken leg?" I decided I would ask Sara if she would like to eat lunch with me today.

Chapter 4
New Friendships

Sara was already sitting down at the table in the cafeteria and was waving to me to join her. She had another girl sitting with her named Angela who has been her friend for a long time. After filling my tray with food, I passed by BreAnna and Jake and said to them, "I'm having lunch with Sara today so I'll catch you later." They didn't seem to have a problem with this; as a matter of fact, they barely had time to acknowledge my existence.

Sara introduced me to Angela and I said, "Nice to meet you; I've seen you in class." Angela said, "Nice to meet you, too. That meatloaf is really good; sorry I started eating before you sat down, but I was starving. I have gym third hour and I really work up an appetite."

This is going to work out great; these girls are so down to earth and it feels great to be included in a conversation again. Sara has long blonde hair and really nice skin. Angela, on the other hand, has brown hair and awful skin, but she is actually prettier than either Sara or me. We had a lot of small talk but just before the lunch hour was over, Sara invited me to come over Saturday night to a party she was having. Things were rolling very fast with these new friends. That was great because I was starting to feel excited about life again. Sara and Angela seem to be a good fit for me and I hope I fit with their friends at the party.

Well, lunch was over and as I passed by BreAnna on my way out of the cafeteria she asked, "How was your lunch with your new friends and please don't forget about me." All in the same breath; that told me she doesn't want me to replace her. It felt great to know she still values my friendship. After all, she is my best friend.

It has been a very eventful day and my whole outlook on life has changed. I made new friends so easily that all the sadness suddenly lifted like a window shade being pulled up that lets in the light. I caught myself smiling as I walked down the hall. Life felt good again.

When I arrived home from school, my mother said, "You seem to be in a much better mood today." I said, "Yes, indeed; what a difference a day can make."

I've learned a valuable lesson today. I learned that I'm responsible for my own happiness and I must deal with difficult situations when it's my happiness at stake. I found new friends and I still value my friendships with both BreAnna and Jake. The focus on being left out of the loop is lessened and now that BreAnna is aware I may have a new set of friends, she is taking notice.

Sara called me to give me the address and time of the party. I don't know a lot of the kids who will be there, but that just means it's time to turn on the charm and get to know them.

The party turned out to be in Sara's garage and driveway. It was kind of like a street dance – actually a driveway dance – with refreshments in the garage. All parents were invited but mine already had other plans. Sixteen teenagers showed up as well as three sets of parents, including Sara's. The only people I knew were Sara, Angela and Zack. Sara was too busy entertaining all her guests and Angela was talking to some guy so I started gravitating toward Zack. He had a friendly smile that put me at ease. "Hey, Chelsea. I heard you were coming. Glad you could make it," Zack said. Zack was a rangy kind of country guy with a shaved head. This shaved head is going to take some time getting comfortable with. The only bald-headed people I know are old people. Zack seemed to be proud of his bald head because he continually rubbed his hand over it. That, or I made him uncomfortable by staring at it; not on purpose, but my eyes just seemed to jump in that direction.

Zack told me that Sara has a way with words and this is what brought them together as friends. Then he asked how I became friends with Sara. I told him the whole scenario about being left out by BreAnna and Jake and needing to find new friends and how I'd asked Sara to have lunch with me. And, of course, that she'd asked me to this party. Zack said, "Welcome aboard. Would you like to dance?" I said yes and was soon having the time of my life. Zack was a great dancer and I'm not too bad myself. We looked better than anyone else at the party. It was as if we could read each other's next move. Angela and her boyfriend were making their way down to our end of the driveway. They started smiling and bumping into us on purpose. It was all in fun and just heightened the joy I was feeling. We danced a couple of other dances and it was time for a break.

As we walked back into the garage to grab a drink, Angela introduced me to her boyfriend; his name is Brad. The four of us had a drink and some chips and talked awhile but the next thing I knew, we were headed back to the driveway to dance again. Brad grabbed my hand and Zack grabbed Angela's; I glanced back at Angela with a questioning look. She winked at me and nodded her approval. I didn't want to cause any waves with my new friends. Brad was not as good a dancer as Zack, but at least he had hair. Brad tried to do things like break dancing but he looked silly because he wasn't very good at it. What's important, however, is that he was having a good time. We danced five in a row; the next one was a slow dance and we switched back to our original partners. Just as Zack grabbed my hand and pulled me toward him, I caught a glimpse of two guys sneaking around the edge of the garage and toward the back fence; they seemed to be trying to hide something but then I saw they were just starting to smoke. My attention had been diverted toward the backyard but when Zack pulled me closer that brought my thoughts back to our dancing. He was telling me what a good couple we made on the dance floor. I must agree; we did outshine everyone. Zack was holding me close and taking big steps; I was floating in his arms. He was by far the smoothest dancer I have ever danced with. There is just something about this guy I really like.

The party was winding down and Sara came over to us to see if we were having a good time. "I apologize for not spending more time with you," Sara said, "but I had a lot of guests who have never been here before and I needed to make sure everything went smoothly." Zack looked at me and said, "We had a great time and I like your choice in new friends." This was truly one of the nicest evenings I have spent in a long time.

Sara asked us to stick around even though most of her guests were leaving. She asked if we wanted to watch a movie in her house and finish off the drinks and chips. Angela and Brad were staying later also. It sounded like a good idea, so we did. After the movie I called my mom to pick me up. On the drive home I told my mom what a great time I had and how I made a lot of really nice friends. It was just really good clean fun. My mom told me it was good to have a variety of friends. I never told her about the situation with BreAnna, but moms have a way of knowing when something is not quite right.

Well, it's Monday morning and school has started. I have a whole new attitude with a whole new set of friends. It just feels good and adventurous to explore life with new friends.

In spite of the remembered good time, I kept recalling the two guys sneaking off to the backyard; no one had talked about drugs or anything, but there was just something about the way they went to the back. I know it takes time to really know if someone is the right fit for you; the more time you spend with them the more you will learn about how they think. I'm not easily influenced, but I certainly would not want to fall into a group of self-destructive, drug-induced, socially transmitted behavior patterns. A lot of kids that do that sort of thing wind up in jail later in life. I don't want that. I have spent a lot of time developing a social, moral, and intellectual mindset so I can live the All-American dream when I grow up. Though I really had enjoyed Sara's party and her friends and the time hanging out watching the movie, the more I thought about those two boys, the more I knew I needed to know more of what she thinks about important stuff. While we were at lunch I invited Sara to my house so we could get to know each other better as well as to provide a private opportunity to talk with her about the guys smoking at her party.

That evening Sara talked about what a great time she had throwing a party and watching her friends have fun. Talking about the party was just the opportunity I needed to let Sara know about those two smoking guys. When I told her, she said she hadn't invited them but they were friends of friends and she would find out just what was up with those guys. This was a relief, because the more I'd thought about their sneaky appearance the more anxious I'd become that I might have fallen into the wrong set of friends for me.

I consider myself somewhat of a preppy; you know, one whose dress and manner are traditional and conservative, and Sara looked the part as well. I asked her if she considered herself a prep and she responded, "You mean you can't tell?" I guess that meant she is a prep. I didn't want to push the issue any further but I will continue to observe her actions and choice of friends.

Next we talked about our school and what a great bunch of kids go there and how lucky we are to live in a district where good teachers work. Sara told me she is very concerned with the political structure of the United States and that the combined class of government and debate works out great for her. She said, "Mrs. Smith is great at encouraging us to express our viewpoint plus she teaches us how to do it more effectively. Because of her, I actually believe I can make a difference for the future by convincing other students about what I think are bad laws."

As I listened to Sara's enthusiasm for preserving people's rights, I was really impressed by the fact that she seems so far ahead of her time. Most of the kids at school put off thinking about politics until they are old enough to vote. It also became pretty clear Sara was using her debate techniques to recruit me into her club of putting people before laws.

Next we talked about Zack. I told her how much I'd enjoyed dancing with him and getting to know him a little better than what I knew from class. "Zack's my best friend and he is as passionate about the negative impact of some laws as I am," Sara said. I said, "I know. When he talked about gun laws and how that could impact his family, his passion was evident. But when I watch him and listen to him talk about guns and hunting, it is the sense of masculinity that stresses attributes such as courage, virility, aggressiveness and domination that attracts my attention to Zack. I've never known anyone quite like him and I'm definitely going to get to know this guy better." When I listen to him talk about his bird or deer hunting experiences he actually transfers his feelings and thoughts to the point I can feel his excitement. Thinking about it makes me want to get a camouflage outfit so I can blend into the natural surroundings and go hunting.

Zack and Sara both make a lot of sense when they talk about city slickers voting on laws that concern country people. City slickers have never had the experience of hunting so they don't understand it. If a law concerns changing the way things are done, it should be voted on by people who understand it or it should not be voted on at all. It's clearly not fair if city folks are allowed to change the lifestyle of country folks just because they outnumber them.

Until I took this government class, none of these things ever even crossed my mind. Now I know the importance of being aware and the need to keep politicians in line.

The constitution of the United States is a system of fundamental laws and principles that prescribe the nature, functions, and limits of an institution, as a government. We as a people must protect this way of life that our forefathers set in place for us to pursue – a state of freedom and happiness. We must be aware and become active in politics to protect our rights. Sara and Zack have given me a whole new meaning of life by exposing me to having a passion for a cause. I'm going to look deep inside myself to find my why for living. In other words, I need to find what is really important to me and start fighting to preserve it by making others aware.

Chapter 5
Going Hunting with Zack

The camouflage outfit that belongs to Zack's mother is really way too big for me, but with a belt around my waist and tissue stuffed into the toe of her boots, I will be fine. Zack's father, Dr. Hughes, handed me ten shotgun shells to put in my pockets. Then he handed me a shotgun; that gave me an uneasy feeling. I had no confidence in myself. Could I pull the trigger? The only things I have ever killed are insects; now I am about to go hunting for quail. A quail is a small chick-like bird with mottled brown plumage and a short tail. If I get lucky and shoot some quail, that's what we'll be having for dinner.

Zack did some fast talking to put this hunting trip together. His dad is really impressed with how quickly I caught onto how to carry a shotgun and load it with shells. Zack gave me some pointers on how to handle myself around his dad and that has really paid off. His dad thinks I'm a natural with a shotgun, when in reality it's the first time I have ever had one in my hand that I was going to shoot.

We loaded up in the pickup and the bird dog, Molly, jumped in the back. Molly is an English Pointer bred for hunting. She is approximately 26 inches in height at the shoulder and weighs about 55 pounds. She is white with liver-colored spots and a flesh-colored nose. Her hair is short and dense and therefore needs little grooming. Zack refers to

Molly as a true friend because of the loyalty she shows him as well as to her work of hunting birds.

Zack's dad is a doctor of bones and joints and hunts on a regular basis with several other doctors of medicine. They have a hunting lease on a 600-acre farm and hunt quail in early winter every year. When we arrived at our destination, there were five men and two other dogs getting ready to go hunting. As we were getting out of the truck one of the men asked, "How's your bitch doing? Do you think she can teach my pup how to point?" Zack's dad replied, "If the pup's capable of learning, Molly's the one you want to help teach her how to point." It sounds so crude to me for these doctors to refer to their dogs as bitches, but it is the proper definition of a female dog. Zack could tell by looking at me that I was offended by the language. He said, "You'll get used to this kind of talk by the end of the day, I promise."

We split up into two groups and headed into the tall grass to hunt for dinner. The doctor with the pup joined our group and the pup was right behind Molly mocking her every move. Suddenly Molly stopped in her tracks, held up one of her front legs, and her tail was straight up in the air; she has found some birds. The pup was shadowing Molly and both were still as a mouse. Suddenly the pup charged into the grass and a flock of quail rose into the air. The quickness of their movement was startling. It sent a sudden mild shock through my body. I could feel the wind from their wings on my face; they were that close. Zack was standing next to me and raised his shotgun into the air, removed the safety and pulled the trigger. Black smoke filled the air and the sound was deafening. I automatically squatted and was sitting on my heels before I knew it. Two more rounds went off, fired from Zack's dad's gun and his friends as well. I jumped as each round was fired. The guys looked down at me and Zack asked if I was okay. I slowly stood up as the smoke cleared and they all started chuckling as a smile appeared on my face.

Molly came running toward us with a bird in her mouth. She went straight to Dr. Hughes, and he put his hand out and Molly softly dropped the quail in his hand. Molly then returned to the grass to retrieve more quail. Dr. Hughes put the quail in a leather satchel hanging from his shoulder. As Molly returned with another quail, the pup was right on her heels with a quail in her mouth as well. The difference was she did not know who to give it to. She brought it to each of us but would not release the bird. It was a game to her. She finally settled down and went to her owner. He had to pry open her mouth to get the quail out. A birddog is supposed to hold the bird in its mouth gently to avoid bruising the meat. Looks like this pup will need some more training.

The three men decided I needed some more coaching. It was agreed by all to let me shoot first the next time we came across a covey of quail. They also decided that before we came across more quail I must shoot my shotgun so I will know how it is done. Zack coached me on how to hold the gun. "You bring the gun toward the sky and rest the wooden part on your shoulder and fire," he said. When I pulled the trigger, the shotgun bumped my shoulder with a hard thud. It was a unanimous vote that I was ready for the next covey of quail. This was exciting, for I had never fired a gun in my life.

Well, off we went into the tall grass to find the next covey of quail. The dogs had their noses to the ground hunting for the birds. We must have walked a mile before the dogs stopped to point. The gun had become heavy and my shoulder was starting to hurt. It's important to relax when you pull the trigger so it won't hurt you. I hope I'm able to do this.

We have caught up with the dogs and they are holding their point. Zack is motioning me to keep walking. We are going to flush the birds ourselves because the dogs are frozen in the point position. We all held our shotguns pointing toward the sky as we went past the dogs to flush the quail. My heart was beating so hard I swear I could hear it. I knew with each step the birds would suddenly fly, and they did. I screamed and pulled the trigger at the same time. The guys fired after me. There must have been thirty quail fly at one time and we shot our fair share. The dogs brought back 22 birds for a total of 37 quail. That will be enough for supper once we add a couple of vegetables.

We walked for another thirty minutes and decided to call it a day. I was so glad because the gun was getting heavy. I was switching it from one hand to the other, but that was no longer helping. I finally asked if we could stop and rest for awhile. We all rested our shotguns on the ground and reminisced about the day's events. Dr. Hughes asked me to describe in detail what I thought about bird hunting. I started off with what a good feeling it was to be in the great outdoors. Just the smell of fresh air and the grasses as we all walked through them spurred my senses. Watching the dogs work the field and finding the birds just through smell was amazing to me, as well as the way it was just a natural thing for the dogs to point to where the birds were hiding. And the most exciting thing is when the quail left the ground right in front of my face. I don't know if I will ever not jump when that happens. They all started laughing at me and then I started laughing with them. The most rewarding part is when the dogs bring the birds to us and we see the results of the day.

Dr. Hughes said, "I think you are a natural born hunter and look forward to hunting with you in the future." This made me feel like part of the group. I definitely would want to do this again.

The break was over and we were heading for the truck when a doe and its fawn were standing right in front of us. Everyone stopped in their tracks and just watched enthralled at the beauty of these animals. Suddenly the doe and the fawn took off running. We all started walking again without a word being spoken.

The truck was a welcome sight. The other party was already there splitting up the birds. Dr. Hughes shouted, "Looks like you guys made a big score." Someone shouted back, "We must have at least a hundred birds here."

After everyone chatted about what a good day it was for hunting, we all loaded up in the trucks and headed for home. Dr. Hughes invited me for supper, so I called my parents from my cell phone and asked if it would be all right with them. They said it was okay as long as I was with Zack's parents and was home by midnight. This was good news because I looked forward to having quail for supper.

As we pulled in front of Zack's house, his mother stepped out and asked if we had enough quail for supper. Zack told her we had enough for two suppers. Zack was in charge of preparing the quail for his mother to cook. He put a big pot of water on to heat up. He told me that sometimes he skins the quail and sometimes he puts them in hot water so the feathers would come off easily. If you leave the skin on they just taste better, and he wanted this dinner to be the best.

Zack had the water boiling hot and took it out to the back porch to clean the birds. He removed the head and craw first. Then he broke the legs off at the hock, cut open the belly and pulled out the insides. Now the bird is ready to be submerged in water, or dunked. Somehow the hot water made it really easy to get the feathers off. I helped remove the feathers but Zack did the removing of the extremities or appendages, whatever you want to call them.

After the birds were cleaned, we took them to Zack's mother for cooking. She had prepared a cornbread dressing to stuff inside the birds. It consisted of dry cooked cornbread, onions, celery, sage, salt, pepper, and chicken broth. She stuffed each bird until the stuffing was coming out of the craw hole. Then she placed them in a baking pan and basted them with melted butter. She put them in the oven and occasionally pulled them out to baste again. She told me the secret to really good birds is the seasoning to enhance the flavor of the quail, and basting it with butter every fifteen minutes.

Mrs. Hughes asked me if I would mind making a salad while she fried some potatoes with onions. "Yes, Ma'am. I would love to help," I said. She gave me a pleased smile and pointed to the refrigerator. I grabbed a head of lettuce and two tomatoes. I always wash my vegetables before cutting them up. Mrs. Hughes took notice and gave me another pleased smile. After the salad was together I started putting ice in the glasses and heated some water to make tea. After the tea sat for five minutes, I added my sugar. It always seems to make better tea when the sugar is added to the hot tea. After the sugar dissolves, it is added to the cold water and stirred. I then put napkins on the table with forks and knives. This whole experience is heartfelt. I'm so energized from this experience - from bringing home supper to helping clean the birds, to making a salad, tea and setting the table.

The smell of quail and cornbread dressing has filled the kitchen. It is heavenly. Dr. Hughes entered the kitchen and said, "By the smell of things, supper must be ready." Well, he was right. Mrs. Hughes was pulling the quail out of the oven and putting two on each plate. Zack was the first to sit down at the table. The rest of us soon followed suit. I sat next to Zack and his mother was on the other side of me. We all joined hands and Zack thanked God for the food on our table. Afterwards, Dr. Hughes said, "It is a family tradition for the children to give thanks for the food on the table as soon as they are old enough to talk. Zack's sisters would take turns with him when they were living at home. Hopefully, now that they are in college, they have continued to give thanks. What children learn when they are young usually stays with them a lifetime. Their mom and I have made a great effort to give our children a platform to stand on with the base being of righteousness and thankfulness."

My first bite of the quail was so tender it almost melted in my mouth. The meat was white, like a chicken breast, but so much better. The stuffing had the flavor of the quail and the quail had the flavor of the stuffing. It is truly delicious to taste or smell. I hope it's okay if I ask for a third bird. After all, I'm a growing girl.

Just to think that this morning when Dr. Hughes handed me a shotgun, I had an uneasy feeling about eating quail I would shoot; it has amazed me at what a difference a few hours can make. This has been one of the most exciting days of my life.

After dinner I helped Mrs. Hughes do the dishes. She made comments about what a good job I did filling her boots. I told her that I had to put tissue in the toe of her boots in order to fill them. We both laughed. I knew she meant that I was a good hunter. I told her she had an amazing family and I hoped I could do as good a job with my family when I grow up. I let her know how much I appreciated the chance to see this side of life. Hunting had never entered my mind until I met Zack. Now I want to do this every year. I want my future family to know this part of life. It just feels so right.

Mrs. Hughes said, "This is a great life and we need to protect the Second Amendment if we want to keep the right to hunt. The Second Amendment is the right to bear arms and was ratified on December 15, 1791. It states that a well-regulated militia, being necessary to the security of a free state, the right of the people to keep and bear arms, shall not be infringed."

I have been studying the constitution in school and I know the first ten amendments are commonly known as the Bill of Rights; however, I cannot quote any of them like Mrs.

Hughes can. The Second Amendment has taken on a whole new meaning to me after today, and I plan to commit it to memory and be able to quote it like Mrs. Hughes.

I now understand where the positive energy comes from that Zack emits when he talks about the importance of protecting our rights. It is the right to provide food for your family as well as protect your family. After all, family is all we really have in life. Friends are great but they just come and go.

I said to Mrs. Hughes, "I hope to have the opportunity to hunt again. God will lead us in the right direction if we just listen to him. My eyes are seeing things the way God meant for them to see. I vow to never cringe in fear of pulling the trigger on a gun to feed a family." Mrs. Hughes replied, "You really should plan on going turkey hunting for Thanksgiving dinner." I said, "It's a date; I will have my own camouflage outfit with boots by then so you will be able to go with us. By the way, thanks again for the loan."

This day has been a very valuable lesson for me. I will never pass judgment on someone because of the way they look. Because Zack had a bald head and a passion for guns, my first thoughts of him were that he was weird. He is anything but weird. This country was founded upon the right to bear arms to protect your family and provide food for the table by hunting game. We must protect ourselves from those who want to take these rights away.

"Hey, Chelsea, how about a lesson on new laws in England? They managed to take away the rights of individuals to fox hunt. This has been a long-lived tradition in Scotland and became illegal in 2002 and in England in 2005. Fox hunting is where a fox is turned loose and a group of hound dogs chase him. The people ride horses behind the hounds and join in the chase. The fox is smarter than the dogs and I have never heard of one getting caught that was healthy. It's all just a very fun tradition that these people have been robbed of by bad laws. You see, lobbyists have a disproportionate amount of influence over people making changes to laws. In other words, they have the time to devote to change laws in a way beneficial to those they represent. This is just another example of what is happening worldwide," Mrs. Hughes said.

What I learned from this is that people who lose the right to hunt are essentially alone with their anguish over the loss of their hobby. You can't see pain or measure its intensity, but you know these people have been robbed of their joy and their sport. This needs to stop and the only way is to make people aware of the damage being done. This is a good example of where city slickers should not be able to vote on country issues. They cannot relate.

It's getting late, and time for me to head for home. Mrs. Hughes gave me a hug and told me how much she enjoyed my company. I hugged her back and told her this day would be with me for a lifetime; that today I learned a new kind of love – the love of hunting. She hugged me tighter and kissed me on top of my head and told me I was always welcome.

I loaded up in the truck and sat between Zack and his dad. They talked about the new pup bruising some of the birds and how she needed some one-on-one attention to break this bad habit. Men have a whole different way of communicating than women do. At times, I felt like they did not acknowledge that I was sitting right there between them. They just talked over the top of my head. Oh well, this is just how men are.

When we pulled into my driveway, suddenly they became aware of my presence. They told me I have potential to become a great bird hunter some day if I continue to indulge in the sport. I let them know that with their help I would, and we said our goodbyes and goodnights.

Chapter 6
Time to Debate

After such an exciting weekend with Zack and his family, it was time for school once again. My government combined with debate class is becoming my favorite. Today the debate is on young people under the age of eighteen sending pornographic pictures over their cell phones. A pornographic picture is intended to arouse sexual excitement and is against the law. The debate is about what the charges should be. Should a young person be charged with a sex offender charge or should it be a lesser charge?

Sara believes the parents should be charged with neglect and Angela believes after the age of awareness – age twelve – you are responsible for your actions. This is going to make for a very interesting day. Something has to be done to keep young people in line.

Our teacher has us come to the front of the class and we must be six feet apart when we debate. I think the six-foot rule is so the teacher can get between the two before things get too far out of hand. Since Sara and Angela are best friends we should not have that problem today.

The teacher flips a coin to see who gets to start the debate. Angela took tails and when the coin was flipped, it landed tails up. Angela began by informing Sara that pornography is harmful and degrading to the moral or intellectual character of our youth and must carry a very harsh punishment to the one committing the act. Sara, on the other hand, believes that charging a minor with being a sex offender is extremely stern and severe for our young people.

Sara said, "Parents who give their child a cell phone with the capability to send pictures are responsible for what that child sends over that phone. If parents have not instilled the morals in their child to deal with a picture phone, then the child should not be allowed that technology on the phone. In my opinion, the parents should be charged with neglect and the child should be ordered to get counseling for a full year."

Angela replied, "If the child is twelve years old or older, he or she should be responsible for their own actions. There should be a charge against them that stays on their record until the age of eighteen. People need to be protected against the actions of someone sending pornography over cell phones. I don't think they should be labeled as a sex offender because those are really bad acts against the innocent and should have their own label. The country needs a whole new label for the crime of sending pornography over cell phones. We could call it a visual offender. People would know the difference in the act, but they need to know that a person is a visual offender. After the age of eighteen the record should be cleared but if this action continues, they should be charged as adults, and then the record never goes away."

Sara replied, "Young people sometimes do stupid things and I believe you could ruin their lives by charging them with a crime that everyone could find out about. If it is going to be posted on the internet for everyone to see, they should at least get a second chance. I think that the first time it happens the parents should be charged with neglect of a visual offender. This way, others can protect their children from an offending child but the parents bear the shame. If, however, the crime is repeated, then the child should bear the shame, have counseling, and do a year's community service. I just think they need a second chance."

Angela replied, "Sara, I will meet you half way on this;

at age sixteen young people should be held accountable for their actions even if it is the first time. If they are old enough to hold a job, they are old enough to bear the responsibility for their actions. If a young person is age twelve to fifteen their name needs to be known in order to protect the innocent. All should have counseling and do community service; this includes the parents. You can remove the names of the young people age twelve to fifteen only if it is one offense."

Sara replied, "Thank you, Angela, for having an open mind. It is nice that we could compromise and come up with a solution. We have to be forgiving of the young, age twelve to fifteen. You have a point with young people age sixteen to eighteen being responsible enough to hold a job so they should also be responsible for their actions with a cell phone. The courts should decide how much damage was done and exact a penalty accordingly. A judicial decision could determine the degree of punishment to be inflicted on the convicted person according to how grievous the crime was."

That was a great debate. The subject is real to life for teenagers today. The access to cameras on a cell phone makes it too easy to get in trouble. It can happen too fast. In my parents' day, you would have to take a picture, wait for it to develop and could only distribute it to a few people; now, with just the click of a button, the whole world could have access. It's just a different world nowadays.

On my way to lunch I thought about how the schools need to be teaching our youth about laws that could change their lives forever. It could become part of a history class, since these kids are making their own history. Your history never goes away and students need to know this.

On my way to lunch I passed Jake and BreAnna's table and waved at them. They are still my best friends, but now other things occupy my mind. The pain of seeing them together no longer exists. I feel happiness for them. My new friends have filled the void that caused my pain.

Just as I sat down at the table, Zack arrived with his tray and sat down beside me. Sara and Angela were already sitting at the lunch table laughing it up. They had a great time debating each other and were completely happy with their solution. I told Sara and Angela they made class very interesting today. It's a touchy subject requiring tact and skill to maneuver around the life of your peers who may not think it is such a bad thing. We don't all think alike.

Angela said, "You know, Chelsea, you are absolutely right. I know a girl on my block who is a senior and she tells me that she and the boy she is dating send risky pictures to each other over their cell phones all the time. What would happen if they broke up and sent these pictures to everyone in school? It would be pretty embarrassing as well as against the law. She is taking a big chance, but she doesn't want to be told that. She doesn't want to think about the consequence of her actions. He has some kind of a spell over her. She does whatever he wants. I think someday she will regret doing this, because all these pictures are stored on a mainframe somewhere in the computer world; they never go away."

Sara said, "You are so right, Angela, and they know exactly where they are coming from. By they, I mean the cops. They can track them down to the exact time they were sent. To be a young kid just thinking you were having fun, things can sure turn out badly for you in the future. If you have a record saying you are a sex offender, it will be very hard to find a job. Employers are responsible for whom they hire and they all do background checks before they hire anyone. If you owned a company, would you hire a sex offender? Young people better consider what their future could be like if they were caught sending pornography over their cell phones."

Sara is right about the future employment of young people; they really need to think about the consequences of their actions. That which logically or naturally follows from their action will be with them for the rest of their lives.

Sara went on to say, "My good friend, Kyle, was telling me about one of the teens in his school who walked into the girls' locker room after gym and snapped a shot with his cell phone of girls showering. He then sent it to his buddy, not knowing his buddy would send it out to the whole school. Next thing you know, the parents of these girls are filing charges against both boys. I don't understand how someone with the exceptional intellectual and creative power that the students of that school have could do something so stupid. Not just anyone can go to Kyle's school. You have to be a freaking genius."

Angela said, "Being intellectually gifted and having maturity are two different things. This sounds like teens trying to have fun. I must admit they have a very strange way of having fun. It is such a waste of their lives. How could they not know that the parents of these girls would find out about their actions? If I was a parent and someone did this to my child, I would have to press charges. Parents are supposed to protect their children. It is the natural thing to do."

She continued, "This could cause long-term damage to some of the girls in the photo. School is supposed to be a secure place for young people; it is the school's responsibility to provide that security. In the future, a security guard should be placed in front of the door to protect the young people from this ever happening again. This may sound extreme, but look at all the lives that have been affected by this vile act. These girls will have a difficult time feeling safe for a long time; some may never get past this event."

Angela is so right about the girls having a difficult time getting past the whole school seeing them naked; they would have to be feeling defenseless and vulnerable for a long time. This sexting crime against them may well be with them for the rest of their lives. It would be difficult for me to walk down the halls of my school knowing everyone had seen me without clothing covering my body. I can see me now, begging my parents to let me change schools where no one knows me. Or, I might beg to be homeschooled. Facing all my peers would be very difficult – not knowing what they were thinking; were they seeing me in that photo or were they seeing me as a person in my clothes? That is what my mind would be doing to me.

Even though the teens that sent these nude pictures are extremely intelligent, their frontal lobes are clearly not developed. We need to segregate them from society and provide them with specialized attention. Juveniles require this to become responsible citizens in the future. I would hate to see their lives wasted with a label of sex offender because their frontal lobes lack development. I personally think picture phones should not be allowed in school. A teen's frontal lobe, the largest part of the anterior portion of the cerebral cortex, is just not ready for picture phones.

Zack looked at me and said, "What's your passion, Chelsea? When are we going to see you debate?" I glanced at Sara, Angela, and then back at Zack and said, "I have given this a great deal of thought and the freedom of speech is very dear to my heart. It falls under the first amendment, which was ratified on December 15, 1791. It states that Congress shall make no law respecting an establishment of religion, or prohibiting the free exercise thereof, or abridging the freedom of speech, or of the press; or the right of the people peaceably to assemble, and to petition the government for a redress of grievances."

Zack said, "Wow, that was a mouthful. I'm impressed that you can quote the first amendment verbatim. Not many kids our age can do that." I said, "If I intend to debate in front of the whole class I want to know my stuff. If I lose a debate, it won't be because I didn't do my homework." Zack said, "I think a debate with you would be interesting; I might learn something." I said, "Bring it on. We might both learn something."

I like the idea of debating a friend because Zack would never embarrass me in front of the class. He would let me down gently so as not to hinder my ability to debate in the future. Debating is something you need to get a feel for slowly if you are timid and shy, like me. Zack would never cause me to feel self-conscious or distressed like some of the other students do to each other. As I get more comfortable in front of the class, I will be able to take on some of these bullies. But for now, I like the idea of being safe.

The next day in class the debate began. I won the flip of the coin, so I began the debate. I turned to the class and said, "I would like to share my passion for the freedom of speech, which falls under the first amendment of the United States Constitution. To me, there is nothing more important to the people than being able to gather in numbers to protest in a peaceful manner so politicians can hear the voices of the people. Most of a politician's time in office is spent with lobbyists or special interest groups who are trying to buy their votes. Working people don't always have the time to represent their views to politicians because they are busy working to make a living for their families while the lobbyist is getting paid to sway Congress to vote for what is favorable to their cause. When we see our rights being stolen from us because of this process, we have a right to assemble in a peaceful group to have our voice heard by the entire nation. Class, that is what I hope to open Zack's eyes to in this debate."

I then turned to Zack and he had a smile on his face and his eyes were twinkling with pride to be a friend of someone who gave such a good opening presentation. He began clapping his hands and then the whole class joined in. I felt victory and the debate has only just started.

Zack said, "Chelsea, I totally agree with what you just said, but there is more to the first amendment than just the right to assemble. How about the freedom of religion? With this comes the freedom to not believe in God. An atheist is one who denies the existence of God. Through the court system, the atheist has managed to get the school prayer taken out of the public school system. My parents experienced the freedom to talk about God in school, and pray to God, where our generation is being denied the privilege and right to pray out loud in school. Our teachers are not even allowed to wear a cross with Jesus on it because it may offend an atheist. Our country was founded upon religion. On our dollar bill, the words "In God we trust," say everything we need to know about the United States of America. The courts are letting a small group of people take away our God-given right to pray, even in public schools. If the atheists do not want to pray, that is fine; they don't have to participate. As a nation, we should not have to give up the principles we were founded on for a group of nonbelievers. With both parents having to work to support a family, religion is being put on the back burner. On Sunday, most just want to rest, not go to church. Our children are being left out of God's world. I believe this will be the fall of our great nation."

This is what makes debating so much fun. You never know what will come out of your opponent's mouth. Looks to me like Zack had no argument with the right to assemble, so he took off in a whole different direction and has thrown me for a loop. You see, I totally agree with him on having prayer in school, but this is supposed to be a debate. My only answer is that, in my eyes, he is right. Somehow, I have to bring this back to my original opening in the debate. Well, here goes my rebuttal, or my agreement.

"Zack, this would be the perfect opportunity for like-minded people to gather in numbers to protest the ruling of the courts. With the freedom of speech and the right to assemble in a peaceful manner, this law could be changed. The nation will have to be behind us in unprecedented numbers. We would be saving our values as a nation under God. It is my opinion that if we could come up with a prayer that every religion would approve of, it could happen. If this prayer talked about the one God we all believe in, this could work. The atheists would not have to recite the prayer. The atheist could stand or sit in silence; this is what they did before the law was passed. In the meantime, Zack, you and I and other teens can spread the word of God to those who will hear what we have to say."

Zack said, "Looks to me like we have solved another one of the problems of the United States of America."

I looked at Zack and gave him a nod of approval and a grin came across my face. My heart was filled with joy as I returned to my seat. I conquered my fears of debating today, thanks to Zack. He made me aware that I was quick on my feet with a comeback out of the blue. I can do this again and let my mind do its thing.

When I look at Zack now, I have very fond feelings for him. As I explored those feelings, it was a very close feeling, more than just a friend but not one of a future husband – not even puppy love. Just a love for who he is: an eye opener and a mentor. Love comes in many packages.

Chapter 7
Angela's Life Story

It's time for the weekend and I invited Angela to my house so we could get to know each other better. Sara and Angela are best friends, but Sara was going out of town with her parents to her cousin's wedding.

Angela likes hanging out at the mall and my mom dropped us off and said, "I'll be back at 5:00; please be at this door so I won't have to wait." We waved goodbye and off we went. It's 1:00 now, so we have plenty of time. The first place we went was to a makeup store. Angela has bad skin and packs on the makeup to hide her blemishes. She has great features and really long eyelashes and that makes her beautiful. Her first purchase was a blemish-covering base. Then, she picked up a cake-like face makeup and turned to me and said, "This is my magic potion. With enough of this, my face looks great from a distance. Up close, anyone can tell I have bad skin, but at least they cannot see the redness. I have a couple of other tricks to keep down the size of the bumps. Every night before I go to bed, I drink eight ounces of water with two tablespoons of apple cider vinegar. My grandmother told me about the vinegar making my blemishes smaller. She had problems when she was my age and it helped her. My grandmother said I inherited my bad skin from her. It's a hormone imbalance. A hormone is a substance produced by one organ and conveyed, as by the bloodstream, to another, which it stimulates to function by means of its chemical activity. This condition could be improved through medication, but my grandparents can't afford the medical cost; anyway with time, it should correct itself. I really don't want to put a bunch of medication in my system."

This was a lot of information to consume about someone I hardly knew. On the other hand, I understand the pain associated with bad skin. Angela was consumed with her bad skin problem. She went from makeup to cleansers. Her focus was only on what she could do to cover or improve her skin. The only skin problem I have ever had was on my shoulders. Occasionally, a mild breakout would occur and when this happened I would take a bath with two cups of Epson Salts twice a week and it would go away. Also, the convenience of being able to wear clothes to cover the problem was an option Angela didn't have. I imagined wearing a tank top when my shoulders were at their worst breaking out, and it did not feel good. With these thoughts, I could feel Angela's pain.

It was time to shop for something I wanted now that Angela had spent her whole twenty-five dollars on products for her face. I needed a new pair of sneakers. I love the comfort of a good-fitting tennis shoe; it's like energy fills my body and I just want to take off running, like I do on the basketball court. It reminds me of the good times with BreAnna and the basketball team. It was a good feeling and in my mind I thought of calling BreAnna to get together and share what has been happening in our lives. My new friends have lessened the pain of Jake and BreAnna becoming an item and leaving me in the cold. I'm past all that pain and would like to bring my two sets of friends together. It's amazing what a new pair of sneakers can do to my mind. I must bring my thoughts back to the moment. It's cheating Angela out of the time we are spending together.

My sneakers are a very clean white. I also purchased

some white ankle socks to go with them. That took all my money. It looks like window shopping for the next two hours, which happens to be one of my favorite things to do. You can get a good idea of the new coming fashion statements. It gives me something to start saving my money for. Looks like the new spring colors will be pink and black, a good color combo. I like the layered look with black underneath and pink on top. Angela seemed to be drawn to dark colors. She wears a lot black and brown. It kind of goes with her dark personality. She seems to be depressed a lot.

As we passed a store carrying long evening gowns we stopped for a moment to glance back at them when a man approached us to ask if he could have a moment of our time. We were both taken aback and somewhat startled. He said, "I did not mean to alarm you, but I could not help noticing how beautiful both of you are. I work for a modeling company and would very much like to take some pictures of each of you to see if my boss would like you to pose for the cover of our magazine." I looked at Angela and said, "That is very flattering; can I have one of your business cards." At that moment a cloud of darkness filled the air; this man gave us an evil look, turned and walked away. He had no business card because he was a fraud. His compliment was excessive and insincerely presented to win favor so we would go with him. Angela and I talked about this situation in depth and decided to report the incident to security in case some girl might believe the man, go with him and be hurt. We went into the store that had the long formal dresses and asked the lady working the cash register to call security. A man arrived shortly thereafter and asked us to come to his office to file a report. We agreed, and in the security office the lady sitting at a computer asked us to join her. She was replaying a video of this man with Angela and me in the video. We filled out a report on what transpired with the three of us. The lady playing the video told us we did a very smart thing by asking for a business card and then reporting the incident to security. She said she would keep our contact information if there were ever a need to testify against this man in court in the event he were ever arrested for hurting someone.

When we left the security office we no longer felt like window shopping and just went to the door where my mom was to pick us up. Angela said, "That was so creepy! I think it might give me nightmares. His eyes grew so cold when you asked for his business card; it was ire so strong I could actually feel his anger. Do you think he is a killer?" I told her, "I observed the same anger he was emitting when his eyes turned cold, but I also felt the air I was breathing turn cold at the same time. If we had been alone with him in some room, I believe he could have done great bodily harm to both of us. I have instincts I inherited from my Grandfather. He was Native American. I can feel when something is not right before most people can. My Grandfather once told me a story about his brother who was on his deathbed. Two days before he died, aunts, uncles and cousins showed up on the porch to say their goodbyes. No one had told them of his illness. My mom said she never knew of so many family members. She did not have enough beds for all of them. They must have known this because they brought blankets to sleep wherever there was room. She said there were so many of them they filled the whole house. They all said their goodbyes and talked about the good times they had fishing and hunting with my great uncle. Seeing all these dear family members made my great uncle's passing a joyous event. I truly hope I can be that happy the day I die. Anyway, they somehow sensed he was dying, and I believe I inherited this gift of knowing when something is just not right."

About the time I finished my story of my great uncle, I started having that creepy feeling that guy had given us and, as I turned my head, there he was walking toward us. The closer he came, the creepier it felt. He was staring a cold hole right through us. I felt a direct and continuous passage of his evilness as he drew nearer and nearer. I thought for a moment I might scream, but then he passed through the door and the feeling completely left my body. Angela looked at me and said, "There is something really wrong with that guy." I nodded my head in complete agreement and acknowledgment of the creepiness this man engendered in us. I have a strange feeling the police may be talking to us about this man some day.

My mother just pulled up to the door and we were relieved to see her. On the way home we told her the story about filling out a report with the mall's security office. She was impressed with the way we had handled the situation.

Upon arriving at my house, the feeling of being safe and secure was quite welcome. Angela and I went to my room to look over our new purchases from the mall. Angela just started talking like she was making a formal admission of guilt, a confession. She said, "You know, Chelsea, sometimes I think evil follows me around and tries to get me to join it. My life somehow has been so screwed up. My parents got a divorce and that is when things started happening. My early childhood was wonderful, like a fairyland - a charming enchanting place. I felt safe and secure and loved. We were living the American Dream. My dad sold cars and my mom was a nurse. One day, a very pretty woman bought a car off my dad's car lot and asked him to have a cup of coffee with her. He agreed because it was all part of doing business. She began telling him how attractive he was and how she was drawn to his personality. This is when he started drinking every night. He really liked hearing good things about himself and, next thing you know, my parents were divorced. This woman did not want me to be part of my dad's life so he abandoned me. He withdrew his support, despite the duty, allegiance and responsibility he had taken on when he married my mom and when I was born. This was the first time I looked evil in the eye. The next time evil came my way was when my mother first started taking Methamphetamine because she was so depressed over what my dad had done. Her so-called friend was losing a lot of weight and had tons of energy and asked my mom if she would like to get high with her and forget her problems. Mom chose to give it a try. At first things seemed great for my mom. She had tons of energy and stayed up day and night for days at a time, but at her job others began noticing something was not right with her and they made her take a drug test. She failed the test and lost her license to be a nurse. This was devastating because we could not live on child support alone. My mom got a job working at a restaurant but could not even hold on to that. Next thing I knew, I was living with my grandparents and my mother had become a prostitute; she solicits men with her body in order to buy the meth, which has totally taken over her mind. I overheard my grandparents talking about this, which is how I know. My mother has lost all her teeth and is totally broken down and living in a nursing home now. Her nervous system is stuck in high gear and has been destroyed. She has gone to the point of no return and is a threat to herself as well as to society. The devil entered my parents' lives and took them from me. You know, if you believe in God, then you must acknowledge the existence of the devil as well. He is here on earth and is looking for lives to destroy."

I felt awful for Angela. I had no idea what she had been through. She began to cry and I gave her a hug and started crying myself. That was the saddest story I've ever heard. How could things have gone so wrong in a kid's life? After we had a good cry I said to Angela, "Your parents had a really bad time in life, but that doesn't mean you have to. You are a good person and I know that. Soon you will have your own family and they will know God and you will protect them from the devil because you have seen the face of evil. You will not allow him to touch your future family; I just know this to be true."

We dried off our faces and went downstairs to have dinner with my family. My parents always insist we have dinner as a family. This makes it where we always have an open means of communication so problems can be nipped in the bud. We also have the opportunity to share each other's fun stories. My parents noticed right off that we had red eyes and must have needed a good laugh.

My parents and I have a little sketch we do to get a laugh out of my friends. I say, "Mom, can I have an advance on my allowance?" Mom replies, "You're already backed up until your 25th birthday; how about you start paying back with interest?" It gets a laugh every time we play this little game.

My mom fixed a really hearty meal; after our ordeal at the mall she knew we would need some comfort food. We had fried chicken, mashed potatoes with gravy, green beans, and a peach cobbler for dessert. Mom makes the best fried chicken in the whole universe. She marinates it and then fries it in extra virgin olive oil mixed with two spoons of real butter. Yummy! I think the neighbors could hear the lip smacking from across the street. The peach cobbler had whole wheat crust on the top only. That means you get a tremendous amount of peaches with a crunch of whole wheat sweet crust with every bite. I had whipped cream on top of my peach cobbler and Angela had a scoop of vanilla bean ice cream on top of hers.

After dinner, I started clearing the table and running water to clean the dishes. I always do my part to help with the meals without a rebellious bone in my body. It feels good to be a help; most teens would defy and resist the authority of parents wanting them to do their share of household chores. I have always believed that what goes around comes around; when I have my own family, I expect my children to pitch in and help just like I have. My parents believe in the old-fashioned way to wash dishes – by hand! My mother says it takes just as much time to put dishes in a dishwasher as it does to do them by hand. It usually takes two loads to do them and you have to rinse them off before you put them in the dishwasher; so why not just wash them, rinse and dry them and put them away and be done with it? I don't argue her logic; I just do the dishes.

As I washed the dishes and rinsed them, Angela dried them and put them away. This worked out great because the glasses go first and I point to where they go; then the plates and I point; then the pots and pans and I point. Angela did a great job helping, so I dried and put away the knives, forks and spoons. I gave her a break. Once the dishes were done, we went back upstairs to talk some more.

The conversation started off with how great Angela's grandparents are to her. She talked about how there is a hole in her heart because of the situation with her parents. Both have totally abandoned their responsibility for the child they had together. They even abandoned the responsibility they had to themselves as human beings. Angela had talked a lot about her mom, so I asked her if she talked to her dad very often. This brought out even stronger emotions because her dad just didn't want to see her. Angela talked about the wicked stepmother saying it definitely applied to this woman. She influenced her dad to the point that she doesn't even exist as far as he is concerned. She talked about him having the backbone of a grasshopper for not standing up to the wicked stepmother. She also blames her dad for what happened to her mom and I believe she may even hate him. I can't say I blame her. Angela went on to talk about how her grandparents came to have her living with them.

Angela said, "One day my mother said a gentleman was coming to our house and asked if I would be nice to him. I then asked if she meant he was coming to have supper with us and she said he would be with me in my room. This sent shivers throughout my body. I told her no way, but she continued to try to convince me that I needed to do this to help her.

My mother went to take a bath and I called my grandparents with trembling hands. When my grandmother answered the phone I started to cry. She kept saying, "What's wrong," but my voice was quivering so badly I couldn't make myself clear. She then said, "Honey, I will be there in five minutes." When she came to the door she told me to get in the car. We left without even saying anything to my mom. Grandma knew my mother was messing with meth and had told me if I ever needed her to just call. When I was inside my grandparents' house, grandma called my mother and told her I would be living in her house from now on. My mother told her it was kidnapping and unlawful and my grandmother said she would tell the Department of Human Services what she was trying to do and that she would be arrested. Mother never tried to get me to live with her again.

My grandmother put me in counseling with a great group of doctors. They believe in talking about problems, with or without the taking of pills. They say pills are like putting a Band-Aid on a cut that needs stitches; you need both. They use pills only if there is no other solution and then only for the necessary time. Teens who try to kill themselves need a lot of support; I see this in the group meetings we have. Medication is necessary if talking doesn't help. In other words, you cannot just ask for a pill to make the emotional pain go way. I see the doctors once a week, eat a balanced diet, and run three miles a day. This is what they demand of me, and I totally understand because I feel great most of the time. I'm wearing out my grandparents' treadmill, but they say, "Don't worry about it." Before I started seeing the doctors, I would be depressed a lot; now it happens only occasionally – what would be considered to be the norm. Nobody is happy all the time. My doctors say some people get sad for no reason at all; it's just part of life. Anyway, sorry to lay all that off on you. When I get into a stressful situation, like with that crap at the mall, my mouth just starts talking."

"That's okay. After all, what are friends for? I want you to know that I don't have loose lips; in other words, if you want this story to be told again you will be the one telling it," I said. Angela said, "I so appreciate it, but it's not a big secret or anything. I've learned in counseling it's okay for people to know what my life is all about; after all, it's not my fault. People will just have to accept me for who I am. I don't look for sympathy, but it does help to be able to talk about my life even if it hurts. Talking about it helps me accept the reality of what my life is, and how I can mold my own future. Someday, when I have a family, I will take every step to ensure that we all have a healthy environment. My mom and dad said hurtful things to each other that allowed their relationship to deteriorate. It's the beginning of the end of a family when the verbal abuse begins.

"I blame the wicked stepmother for all my problems, but in reality my father had a choice. He chose her over me. I have not gotten past the fact that he has abandoned me. He has totally withdrawn his support emotionally. I know this is one thing that I will never be able to get past. When I grow up, I will be very choosy when I pick a mate. The one quality I will look for is selflessness – someone concerned about others rather than himself; in others words – unselfish. My father drank a lot of alcohol and this is when my mother and father started saying terrible things to each other. He drank every night. This is something I will avoid in my life. I think alcohol is meant to be done on special occasions only. It can lift the spirit, but what goes up must come down. It's just unhealthy to do every day. I know I sound wise beyond my years, but it's only because I have lived life in a house where evil resided. Without evil, we don't recognize good or appreciate it."

Boy, oh boy, has Angela had some hard knocks in her life. She has opened my eyes to what can happen to people's lives if they don't have their eyes wide open. I feel so blessed to have such a great family. I have learned a lot from Angela's life story. I think I will hug my mom and dad at least once a week for the rest of my life, just to say thanks for a wonderful life. I wonder if Angela would like to go to church with me tomorrow. I think I will ask her.

The sermon was on the Epistle of James, chapter 1, verses 12 through 15. Temptation: "[12]Happy the man who holds out to the end through trial! Once he has been proved, he will receive the crown of life the Lord has promised to those who love him. [13] No one who is tempted is free to say, 'I am being tempted by God.' Surely God, who is beyond the grasp of evil, tempts no one. [14] Rather the tug and lure of his own passion tempt every man. [15] Once passion has conceived, it gives birth to sin, and when sin reaches maturity it begets death."

This part of the sermon hit home to Angela, for she told me her mother fell into temptation of the quick fix meth gave her. Angela referred to meth as the big lie. It gave comfort in the beginning only to steal her mother's life and soul in the end.

The sermon went on to talk about chapter 4, verses 11 and 12: Judging One's Fellows: "[11] Do not, my brothers, speak ill of one another. The one who speaks ill of his brother or judges his brother is speaking against the law. It is the law he judges. If, however, you judge the law you are no observer of the law, you are its judge. [12] There is but one Lawgiver and Judge, one who can save and destroy. Who then are you to judge your neighbor?"

This part of the sermon hit home for me. I really try not to do this but sometimes it just jumps out of my mouth. I always apologize to God and make efforts not to judge people in the future.

It felt great to go to church. It's like sunshine on your face. When you feed your spirit, you fly with the eagles. You just get this natural high like you are with God. It is the ultimate high. Every Sunday after church I have a little prayer; I say, "Everything we see and everything we can't see is because of you. Thank you God for these gifts." This is my little, one-on-one with God, and it makes my heart sing every time I say it. I'm so lucky that my parents have brought me up in the church. I know it will be in my heart my whole life.

I looked at Angela on the way to the car and said, "What do you think about my church?" She said, "I've never been to a church I didn't like. My parents never were churchgoers but my grandparents always took me to church on Sunday. I think if my parents knew God the way I do, none of the bad things they did would ever have happened. The devil was at work with them. It is worse than any horror movie I've ever seen. I guess because it is real life, not pretend. God will be my shield and when I have a family they will know him well.

I feel sorry for any child who does not know God. At my church a bus picks up kids who don't have a way to get to church. Just because their parents don't go to church is no reason why they can't. Everyone in the neighborhood knows if they want to attend, the bus will pick them up."

I feel really good for Angela because she has great plans for her future. I can just imagine her with a husband and a houseful of kids sitting in the front row in her church.

Some people spend their whole life blaming their parents for the way they live their lives - It's their parents' fault they do drugs; it's their parents' fault they don't get along with other people; it's their parents' fault they don't go to church. Angela chose to be responsible for herself even though she has a license to blame her parents for every bad thing she does. Angela has a good heart because she chose that path. We all have a choice over how we live our lives.

Chapter 8
Backyard Croquet

It's time to bring all my friends together for a party so they can get to know each other. BreAnna and Jake see me have lunch with my new friends every day, but they never speak to each other. I think it's time for me to break the ice with a backyard croquet game. Also, since Angela never talks about her boyfriend, Brad, this party will help me get to know him.

It's a beautiful spring morning and I'm putting together some snacks and making sweet tea to drink. I cooked some chickpeas the night before to make some hummus with tahini and fresh spinach. It makes a great spread to put on crackers. For the chips, I mashed avocado, tomato, and onion with seasoning to make guacamole. I put cheese and ham on toothpicks; it makes a great finger food and is so easy to put together.

The first guests to arrive were BreAnna and Jake, with his nerd-type personality. Sometimes teenagers like Jake need someone who is like a sponsor to them – someone who can say by their presence, "This guy's all right." It worked for BreAnna. As a matter of fact, if it weren't for me, they would never have known there was chemistry between them. Chemistry is a mutual attraction, but you have to meet and be introduced before you even know if chemistry exists between you.

Next to arrive was Sara who was escorted by someone I've never seen. She introduced him as Kyle and said he lived in her neighborhood and went to a private school for geniuses. "Kyle has exceptional intellectual and creative abilities when it comes to music. He plays the piano," Sara said. Kyle shook my hand and was turning the brightest shade of red because of Sara's introduction. I then introduced Sara and Kyle to BreAnna and Jake. When Jake was shaking Kyle's hand, he said, "There's always room for another genius; I'm into inventions to save the planet from greenhouse gasses. What type of music do you fancy?" And with that, they were off in their own little world. Sara said, "I knew these two would hit it off when you told me that Jake had the capacity for understanding and knowledge and was a person of great intellectual ability. It sounded like you were describing Kyle." I said, "Sara, you have this ability to make it where everyone can fit in somewhere. Thank you so much for bringing Kyle." With the two guys off in their own world, the opportunity for BreAnna and Sara to get to know each other was at hand. BreAnna said, "You know, Sara, I see you in the lunch room all the time and I'm looking forward to getting to know you."

This is a great start for the party. BreAnna and Sara are really hitting it off and sharing stories about their romantic dates with the genius boys. Jake, who is caught up in his environmental stewardship of saving the earth from human beings, has this same tunnel vision – narrow-mindedness even, when it comes to BreAnna. He can see no other girl in the same light as he sees BreAnna. This makes for a very intense relationship. On the other hand, Kyle, who hopes to be the centerpiece of an orchestra, loves large numbers of people around him. He has images of musicians performing together on various instruments, organized into sections, with Kyle and his piano being the centerpiece. Strangely enough, this is also Sara's personality; she likes being the center of attention and surrounding herself with her friends. Kyle and Sara have the same need to be encircled by large numbers of people while being the center of attention, while BreAnna and Jake seldom have room or even a need for other people. It's funny how people can find each other in this big world.

The next guests to arrive are Brad and Angela. They make a very handsome couple. Angela's grandmother drove them to the party and Angela gave her grandmother a kiss goodbye. That was so sweet. Brad thanked her for the ride; he is so polite and has such good manners. He escorts Angela up the driveway with his hand in the small of her back as if to guide her and give her confidence. Because of all the ill-fated things Angela has been through, it's good that Brad somehow knows how to give her a feeling of assurance and trust. His hand in the small of her back let her know he was there for her.

As they walked up the driveway, Angela waved her hand to get my attention. I waved back as I walked toward them to welcome them to the party. Angela gave me a hug, which surprised me because we haven't known each other for very long; I guess we have shared experiences and very emotional stories together and I feel very close to Angela while she is hugging me. It was a really long hug. Brad just nodded his head to let me know he acknowledged my existence. Brad is very quiet but at the same time demands attention because he is very good looking and built strong as a bull. He has a quiet confidence and self-assurance that speak volumes.

Before I knew it Zack was next in line for a hug. He came out of nowhere. This is the most hugs I have ever had in one day. It's so exciting I can hear my heart beating. Zack grabbed my hand and we walked back up the driveway to join the party.

I introduced those who did not already know each other and then said, "Let the party begin." I put numbers in a hat to draw for what order we would play croquet. This is considered an adult game, I guess, because none of my friends knew how to play it or have even seen a croquet game set. I described how the game is to be played, "The way to play this game is that the players drive wooden balls through a series of wickets using these long-handled mallets. You will pick a color of ball when it is your turn to play. You drive the ball through each of the wickets and you drive away your opponent's ball by hitting your own ball when the two are in contact." Brad drew number one, so he started the game by picking up the ball with a red stripe. Red is a very aggressive color, so we had better all look out for Brad.

It turns out that being a big strong and aggressive brute is not an attribute that is required to win the game of croquet. It requires finesse, refinement and an execution with precise measurement successively repeated within close specified limits of the wickets that the ball must go through. In other words, Kyle took first place and Jake came in second. BreAnna came in third. I only had prizes for the first three winners – dark blue tee shirts, size large, with the words, "I'm a Winner!" printed in white on the front. It worked out great because the game allowed conversation between my friends because of the slow pace of the game. Kyle and Jake replaced their shirts with their new ones, squaring off their shoulders to proudly sport their new labels of "I'm a Winner!" They obviously took great pride in their victories. It gave me a good feeling to see the pride on their faces. BreAnna opted out of changing her blouse because she was already wearing the cutest new outfit that flattered her figure. She thanked me for having the prizes and commented on how good Jake looked in his winner's tee shirt. I told BreAnna, "I understand you not wearing your winner's shirt because it is a size large; maybe you can wear it as a nightgown since it will be so loose and comfy. You could go to sleep knowing you are a winner." She said, "Thanks for letting me off the hook."

Everyone gathered around the picnic table for some tea and snacks. Brad started off the conversation with, "I guess the color red didn't work as an intimidation technique in the game of croquet, seeing how I came in second to the last." Everyone got a laugh out of that statement. Sara said, "If I must say so myself, this is a great game. I've never seen it played or even heard of it until today. Where has it been hiding?" I replied, "It's now a game for the more refined adults." Jake replied, "Who says teens can't be refined?"

After everyone was snacked out on dips and chips and sitting down, it was time for some music. We started out with some slow soul of an easy-listening nature so we could relax. It was a favorite to all of us.

I announced, "It's time for each couple to share an interesting but personal story about themselves. This will be an opportunity for each of us to let everyone present know what is important to us so we can get to know each other better. Since this may be a little difficult for some of you, I'll start and then we'll go in a clockwise direction.

"The thing that I have in common with Zack is that we value our families and believe in the need to protect our freedoms from lobbyists who want to buy them for special interest groups. Now I'm going to pass this stick in my hand to Zack, which means it is his turn to talk," I said.

"As Chelsea told you, we both believe in protecting our freedoms. Well, my passion is hunting and I'm proactive in protecting my rights. I plan to run for a government office some day to protect people's rights. And with that, I pass the stick to Angela," Zack said.

"I'm incredibly strong – that is, spiritually strong. Without my religion, I would be nothing. I came from a very dysfunctional family and have risen above my raising because of my faith in God. My goal in life is to touch as many souls as possible and lead them to the true spiritual light I now live in. And with that, I pass the stick to Brad," Angela said.

"All my life my family has been a loving supportive circle all around me and I try to make them proud in everything I do. I see the problem of drug use as being the downfall of the United States. My plans are to become a DEA agent to protect children and adults from the drug pushers. My family takes in foster children whose parents were doing drugs and were found unfit to raise their children. With this, I pass the stick to BreAnna," Brad said.

"My passion is basketball and when I'm too old to play I hope to coach. With that, I pass the stick to Jake," BreAnna said.

"Someone has to save the world from greenhouse gases, and I hope to invent a machine to capture all the pollution and contamination in the air, soil and water, and with this, I pass the stick to my new friend, Kyle," Jake said.

"I plan to be a concert pianist and create harmony that will change the world in a way yet to be seen. Music is a universal language that is comprehensively broad enough to bring all members of a particular culture into a oneness of the message given. It will be an earth-shattering moment when I bring the world into a oneness, and with that, I pass the stick to Sara," Kyle said.

"The fastest-growing population of homeless people is those who use drugs or alcohol and those with mental health problems. As a social worker, I can make a difference in the life of a lost soul or a broken mind. I have the gift of gab and sometimes that's all a person needs is someone to talk to. I want to use this God-given gift to bring some sunshine into the lives of the less fortunate. And with the baring of my soul, I pass the stick back to Chelsea who never told us what she wants to do with her life," Sara said.

"Well, you are right, Sara. Maybe I should have let Zack start, because everyone followed suit with future plans.

I would like to be a teacher some day. I would like to lead my students by example, and by experiences I have acquired in life. I want my students to know the value of friendship with fellow students and to cherish those friendships because they can provide comfort in life's tough times. I believe there is more to teaching than just what is in the textbooks," I said.

I'm glad we participated in this exercise because it definitely let each of us know something about the others. It's a window into our innermost desires when we share what we want to do with our lives.

The party is going great. This last game opened conversation between all of my friends. They seem to be enjoying each other's future goals and were now discussing them in detail. I'm so blessed to have a group of friends who click with each other.

Sara came up to me and said, "I never knew you wanted to be a teacher." I said, "I always thought teaching is important because teachers can mold the lives of their students. You know, when I first met you, I was extremely depressed and your accepting me into your circle took all the bad feelings away and brought joy back into my life. When I become a teacher, I will demand that my students interact with each other. I will make it part of the learning process. Happy kids just learn better."

About this time, Brad approached me with Angela right behind him and said, "Chelsea, when you become a teacher and I become a DEA agent we will clean up the schools' drug problems together; you just call me any time. I think a lot like you – kids become what they learn in school; they need to know that someone who gives or sells them drugs is not their friend."

BreAnna said, "Okay everyone, listen up. It's time for my favorite game, Limbo. For those of you who have never played the game, it goes like this; it is a West Indies dance in which the dancers bend over backward and pass repeatedly under this broom, which is lowered slightly each time the last person passes under it. Now, let the game begin."

BreAnna always wants to play this game because she is so limber she can almost tie her body into a bow. She knows she has an edge in Limbo and always wants to show off her ability. Everyone made it through the first round and BreAnna was so confident that before the second round began she announced that the last one standing would win the tee shirt she had won in the croquet game earlier. This was an inspiration and incentive to give it your all. Everyone was having a great time with this game and by the fourth time it was lowered, three of the players had already fallen down. By the sixth time the broom had been lowered, BreAnna was the only one left; but, of course, she knew the outcome before the game was even started. She has been playing this game since she was ten years old and she has never lost. Everyone had a great time playing Limbo and the girls were actually better at this game than the boys.

The boys' pride had been damaged and they drifted off and began throwing a Frisbee to each other. My backyard is quite large and they were spread out throwing the Frisbee as far as they could. I must say, they were impressive.

The girls seemed to migrate around the picnic table and were kind of sizing each other up. About this time, BreAnna said, "I like your choice in friends, Chelsea." I replied, "Thank you, BreAnna; now they are your friends as well." Everyone giggled and the bond between friends was sealed.

Sara said, "Looks like Kyle and Jake are really hitting it off. Kyle is new to the neighborhood, and being the socialite that I am, I invited him to this social event of the year to jump start his new life. I can't think of anyone else more deserving of his companionship than me. Isn't he adorable?" BreAnna said, "I'm so glad you brought him because Jake is the shy type but the two of them are really hitting it off. I love to see Jake happy. You know, I'm madly in love with him and want to spend my life feeling the way I do right this minute. It's the most glorious feeling in the world. Jake is magnificent and intelligent and we will have the perfect family."

"Hold on; you're only fifteen years old, girl. Get a grip; you have several years of dating to see if there is someone else out there that is more magnificent than Jake," Angela said. BreAnna replied, "If it got any better than this, I wouldn't be able to stand it."

Well, this is an eye-opener for me; I'm totally freaked out. I knew they were close, but I was unaware they were 'married' close. BreAnna told me earlier today that her relationship with Jake has never gone further than a kiss. I had no idea she was in love until right now. I'm very happy for her, if she is indeed in love, but I have yet to experience the feeling of a getting-married kind of love. To fully understand that feeling, it has to happen to you personally. So far, Zack is just a very good friend who is teaching me a lot about life. I totally think that is all it will ever be. My mother always told me that to love myself is the beginning of a life-long relationship; that you must love yourself in order to understand love and be capable of loving others. I know that I possess the capability to love, but the right person just hasn't come along for me yet. I'm in no hurry to find the man of my dreams; after all, I'm just fifteen and time is on my side.

The guys were on their way to the picnic table for some refreshments. They had worked up a thirst. Jake immediately migrated toward BreAnna and Kyle was right behind him. Jake said to BreAnna, "Someday we will go to a concert and Kyle will be playing the piano in all his glory." Suddenly, Angela said, "I wrote a poem called, 'Let Me Tell You a Story.' Maybe Kyle could help me set it to music." Kyle said, "Let's hear the lyric and I will see if there is something I can do with it." Angela said, "Okay. It goes like this:

> 'Let me tell you a story about the untold Glory.
> If you wait too late, you risk your children's fate.
> Without the state of grace, you won't make the great escape
> out of this world into the next.
> If you lose your faith, your heart will turn to hate.
> God gave you love.
> So use it. Don't abuse it. Don't confuse it.

> Faith is the testimony
> of your forever matrimony.
> If your children are to relate,
> you must translate their fate.
> The first place to start –
> put love in your heart.
> Life is for living/accepting/forgiving.
> Your time on earth is but a blink of the eye
> so try the golden path on which you can rely.
> If you lose your faith, you heart will turn to hate.
> God gave you love
> So use it. Don't abuse it. Don't confuse it.

> Let me tell you a story about the untold Glory.
> If you wait too late, you risk your children's fate."

Everyone stood up and clapped their hands. Someone

hollered, "Good job! You're one of God's angels, Angela." When the clapping subsided, Kyle said, "I definitely think we can do something magnificent with your song because God will be on our side. We will be doing His work." Angela gave Kyle a hug but was at a loss for words. Everyone gave Angela a pat on the back and it was just one of those very special moments that touches everyone's heart.

Kyle said to Jake, "I couldn't help noticing the silver bands that you and BreAnna are wearing. Do they mean you two are together? After all, they are matching." Jake said, "Yes, we are together, hopefully till the end of time. However, the band represents purity. We plan to remove them the day we get married. Having God's blessing is more important to us than the desires of the flesh. Being with BreAnna is the all-time high that I have ever experienced in my life. We would not jeopardize the feelings we have by complicating them with anything more physical. There is a higher level than the needs of the flesh. If the day comes that we can no longer control ourselves, we will get married. Our plans are to graduate high school and, hopefully, college before we marry."

Everyone's jaw just dropped and BreAnna was twisting her silver band the whole time Jake was talking. The whole thing sounded so sweet to me. Jake has a valid point. God's blessing is the most important thing a person could desire. After we die our spirit goes on to infinity, which means unbounded space and time. I hope never to offend God because when people offend God they are offending themselves. Our bodies are the temple of God.

Zack came over and sat down by Jake and said, "You know Chelsea is a really good friend of mine and even though this is the first time I have gotten to know her other friends, I see how you guys are her best friends ever. You two are very special. We all should be so lucky to find someone we want to spend the rest of our lives with."

Zack looked at me and squeezed my hand. We have friendship and we both know that, and respect that friendship. Someday, I hope to have what BreAnna and Jake have but I'm not in any hurry. I look at it like this: I have my whole life for marriage; I want to meet a lot of people and enjoy my youth. When I do marry it will be 'till death do us part.' I believe the Bible is the greatest book ever written and if people can live their lives according to the rules in the Bible, their lives will be blessed, even after life as we know it. The afterlife is where my goals are set.

Brad asked, "Chelsea, what is on the other side of your backyard?" I said, "It is a wildlife refuge. It is for the protection of and a haven for wild animals. If you guys want, we can take a walk through the woods, but Zack, all animals and birds are off limits." Everyone chuckled and off we went.

I have a trail I take at least three times a week that leads to a pond that is my favorite spot on earth. My parents bought a bench and put it at the edge of the water so we can enjoy the wildlife that come to get a drink of water. All of the wildlife are familiar with our scent and know that we do not present any danger, so they do not fear us. It is not unusual to see a doe or a fawn or a buck with a large set of antlers. Sometimes my mom and I tie a piece of bacon to a string and throw it in the water to see who can bring in the biggest crawdad. It's a lot of fun and the crawdads have a great meal.

When we arrived at the pond, Sara said, "Awesome! This is just beautiful. If it was warmer, I would jump in and take a swim." "Well, I guess this summer we need to have a pond party," I said. Brad said, "Let's look at that rope in that tree over there. I bet I could swing out over the water and make it back to the bank without getting wet." Zack said, "Hey, dude, it looks like it is made to drop you off in the deep part of the pond. I wouldn't try it if I were you." Well, you know how guys are. The challenge was on. Brad grabbed the rope and pushed his body out across the water. He swung out over the water and his hands slipped as he was swinging back toward the shore of the pond. The closer he came to the shore, the higher he pulled his feet up so they wouldn't get wet. It just wasn't working. He found himself swinging back out to the middle of the pond because he did not let go at the bank of the pond. This time, when he was swinging back to the shore, he let go but wound up knee deep in water. He started laughing and saying, "This water is freezing." He made his way out and took off his shoes to empty out the water. Then he put them back on and said, "That water will get your attention." I said, "We'd better get back to the house so I can get Brad some dry socks."

We headed back to the house and all my friends were laughing and talking to each other and I felt that my party was so much fun.

When we made it back to the house, I got a pair of dry socks out of my dad's drawer. Brad was grateful and put them on and walked around in socks without shoes. I told him, "In another couple months the water will be warm; if you want to come back for a swim, you are welcome." "I just might take you up on that," Brad said.

Angela got a text message from her grandmother that she was in front on my house and ready to take her and Brad home. This is the end of the party, but the beginning of BreAnna and Jake being part of my circle of new friends.

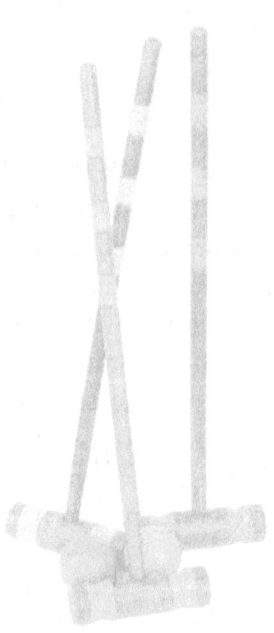

Chapter 9
Reunited

It is a Sunday morning and as I awake, my body is full of happiness. A smile is creeping across my face as I stretch my extremities and flex my muscles in every direction. I have total uncontrolled joy and I love every minute of it. My Saturday party was the best I had ever been to and I hoped my friends felt the same as I do today. My father always tells me that people run in tribes. God blessed me and has given me the best tribe I could possibly find. My tribe consists of jocks, preps and intellectuals. Our values are what bring us together. We all value our bodies, minds and souls. We seek out what life has to offer that will nourish and develop us into what God intended us to be.

I feel badly for the destructive tribe of teens: the ones who take the chance of the self-infected disease called lung cancer by smoking. I look at these teens as being harmful to themselves as well as the others who inhale their secondhand smoke. Then, there are those who smoke meth. They take a chance of addiction that could totally control their lives. Meth is a poison chemical put together by a meth monster in a farmer's field or some dirty building. You don't even know what all is put into this destructive and fatal drug. How could people do that to their bodies? Meth is a substance that causes injury, illness, and even death. It is one of the most destructive drugs a teen can do. It is truly a porthole to the dark and depressing side of life. Anyone who offers meth as a gift is not a friend, but rather the worst enemy one could ever have. They want to steal your health, fry your mind, and stomp on your soul. Friends don't make friends addicts. The devil has his followers just as God does; know this for what it is.

The tribe I belong to worships God but is aware the devil is lurking around every corner. He is always looking for new recruits. He likes to tempt us when we are down. My experience with temptation was when BreAnna and Jake became an item and I felt left out in the cold. I was tempted to crawl in a corner and lavish myself in self pity, and wish bad things to happen to BreAnna and Jake's relationship. Because I know God, those thoughts were put out of my mind and I searched for relief from the pain in a positive way. My blessing was the new group of friends God sent my way. Now He has brought BreAnna and Jake back into my life once again. I truly feel I have been blessed, and I'm enjoying the happiness God has put in my heart.

As I begin reminiscing of the past experiences I have had with BreAnna, the way she told me she was introduced to God comes across my mind. BreAnna's parents were atheists, those who deny the existence of God, but BreAnna asked if she could go to church to make her own decision as to whether God existed or not. BreAnna was only nine years old at the time, but God must have sent her a guardian angel to give her the strength to question her parents' beliefs.

I remember BreAnna telling me about the first time she had met God. She talked about how she took a bath, rolled her hair and wore a dress to God's house; she wanted to be worthy of God. She so wanted Him to accept her.

Her parents dropped her off at the door and pointed to where they would park the car, and told her she did not have to stay for the entire sermon; that she could leave any time she wanted. What a brave little girl she must have been because she stayed for the entire sermon. BreAnna felt God's presence the moment she walked into His house and was filled with the Holy Spirit by the end of the sermon. She felt a glow all around her body, from head to toe. When she got home and looked in the mirror, she saw a light in her eyes that was not there before entering God's house. Her parents continued to drop her off at the church door for a few weeks and some of the church members noticed she was always alone. One of the Sunday School teachers invited her to class and told her about a bus that would pick her up if it was all right with her parents. This fine lady walked BreAnna to her parents' car and made arrangements for the bus to pick BreAnna up and bring her to church and Sunday School in the future.

I think it is an absolutely perfect way to meet God - to find Him because you want to. BreAnna is the most courageous person I have ever met. She will make an impact on this old world in which we all live; I can feel that when I'm around her. I guess it's that light, the Holy Spirit, she received the first day she visited God's house. BreAnna shares her story about how she met God with young people whose parents have left God out of their lives. She tells them how they can contact the nearest church and tell them about their situation. Someone will arrange for them to have transportation to God's house. If all else fails, they can have a personal relationship by just introducing themselves to God and talking to Him daily.

BreAnna always talks about how someday she wants to be a coach and how winning is so important in basketball. But what is more important is for God to win against the devil. Her main goal in life is to bring as many souls as she can to play for God's team. The team playing for God is the winning team and the devil is for losers. Even if a person is not physically strong, mentally they can defeat the devil by being on God's winning team. She always stresses this when the opportunity presents itself. She loves to quote the Bible. One of her favorites is John 8, verse 12, "I am the light of the world. No follower of mine shall ever walk in darkness; no, he shall possess the light of life." She also quotes verse 34, "I give you my assurance, everyone who lives in sin is the slave of sin." BreAnna would say, "Who wants to be a slave? That's not cool." She just has a special way of reaching out to those who need guidance. All of her shyness disappears once she begins to talk about Jesus Christ, and Satan being the prince of darkness.

I was raised in the church and I believe devotedly in Jesus Christ, and I can see that BreAnna someday will be one of the best coaches God ever appointed to coach his believers. BreAnna has a powerful appetite to get the word of God into the hands of those who are in need of spiritual healing. My goal in life is to be a witness to the good works that my best friend, BreAnna, will be accomplishing throughout her life. If the opportunity prevails, I hope to bring the light into souls that are in need of guidance as well. The method I now use is in the form of teaching. I want to share positive learning interaction with the shy souls God has put on this earth. That is how I came to know BreAnna.

I first noticed BreAnna looking at me one day and it seemed as if she wanted to be included in the group of teens I was talking to. I always make an effort to include anyone who shows an interest in the social setting I am engaged in at the time. My mottos are, 'Always be friendly,' and 'If I'm scared, don't show it.' Even though I did not know BreAnna at the time, I waved her over to join in the conversation. She smiled at me and joined the circle of teens.

The conversation was concerning a male classmate who had committed suicide. Everyone was trying to figure out why he had committed such a heinous act. The boy tied a rope around a tree limb that hung out over a creek that had about four feet of water in it. He then tied the other end of the rope around his neck and swung out to the middle of the creek, which broke his neck and paralyzed him. The boy was helpless and unable to move, but not yet dead. The rope was not tied tight enough to withstand the weight of his body and he slipped from the tree, leaving him to drown in the four feet of water. The cause of death was said to be suffocating in a liquid.

We were discussing why he would want to take his own life. Was the decision to end his life determined by his home life or, perhaps, because he was being bullied by a group of classmates, or a combination of circumstances? Sometimes, he would come to school with bruises on his arms and face. He would say he fell off his skateboard. When he came to school with these bruises, he would always be withdrawn for a few weeks afterwards. This made everyone think there was no skateboard accident. A group of punks would bully this boy just for kicks. They saw he was weak, vulnerable and susceptible to attack. This is how animals react in the wild. For heaven's sake, we are human beings. We have souls. What is wrong with these kids?

The bullies have become very quiet since the incident. They all know how they treated the kid and now they have to live with that on their consciences; even they know the difference between right and wrong.

BreAnna suggested that the group of teens hold hands and have a moment of silence. Prayer is not allowed in school, but we have our own code, which is holding hands and passing our spirituality between us for a healing experience. After the group began to break up, I started a conversation with BreAnna. I began by telling BreAnna that I planned to become a teacher some day and that I would be a strict teacher. Bullying would not be allowed. I would keep within specific and narrow limits of the discipline rules. No person should have to endure what those bullies did to that kid. It would never happen on my watch. BreAnna looked at me in surprise. I guess all the ranting and raving wasn't going to change anything. "The past is the past and the boy is dead, but the future can be molded and I plan to be a part of that process. Behind my backyard is a pond with a tree branch reaching out toward the middle of the pond. Years ago, my dad tied a rope on this branch so we could swing out across the pond and drop in with a big splash. I don't know if I will ever look at that rope again without thinking about that boy killing himself with a rope," I said.

"Everyone keeps referring to him as the boy; you know his name is Allen and we should all show him that much respect," BreAnna said.

She was right; somehow, none of us wanted to personalize the event by using his name. It was like we were trying to distance ourselves. If we were to use his name, it would be like engraving it into our souls. We would somehow be unable to maintain our innocence.

This is what I really like about BreAnna; she always forces me to deal with reality. That is actually the only way to get past the negatives that life throws our way – face them head on. I never referred to Allen as that boy again. The pain of knowing someone who committed suicide had taken me to a dark place that I never knew existed. It was truly painful, and I don't think the pain will ever go away when the memory is revisited. The school provided a counselor to discuss all the emotions we would be dealing with and advised us to seek help if we felt it would facilitate lessening the pain. Somehow, talking to BreAnna about the loss of Allen gave me more help than the counselor had. She just has that special gift.

BreAnna told me that if I felt so passionate about people who were being bullied, I should befriend them by behaving as a friend to them. That might include telling them how to deal with bullies or even turning the bullies into the school principal. The principal gets paid big bucks to provide a moral and ethical standard that students should live up to. Also, if a student has friends, it is easier to handle bad situations. Friendship is a very powerful healing tool that every child should have access to in bad times. Friends can help us get past all the pain.

BreAnna taught me a valuable lesson on that day; be proactive when you notice a student is having a difficult time in life. There are teens that live a nightmare of a life and if I can shed a little light in their life then, maybe, they can make it past the bad times. If just one of us had befriended Allen, he might have looked at life as a gift and not the burden it had become.

BreAnna believes that at some point in everyone's life, difficult times will come. During these times, if you have someone to lean on, it is much easier to endure and make it past them. Some people's difficult times are much deeper than others' and BreAnna believes they cannot see any light at the end of the tunnel. They just give up. That must be what happened to Allen. It was all just too much for him.

With some soul searching, I came to the conclusion that had I acted on the bullying that was taking place, the outcome for Allen could have been different. This is why I'm so angry about the whole thing. Somehow I feel responsible for not putting a stop to the bullies' habitually cruel acts against Allen.

I discussed this with BreAnna and she said that all of us had some responsibility in this and that I should lighten my guilt and share it with the rest of the school. We all knew that bullies pick on smaller and weaker people; it's as if picking on someone else will make them feel better about their own inadequacies, shortcomings or failings. No one should be allowed to pour out their problems on someone else, like Allen. We all should take responsibility for protecting one another from that sort of abuse.

Just talking to BreAnna about the problem lightened my heavy heart. I took a vow to never allow what happened to Allen to take place with my knowledge of its occurrence. I plan to be proactive from this day forward.

Allen had left a suicide note on his MySpace page as well as on the door of his home for his mother to find when she came home from work. The note read, "Dear mother, My mood keeps turning darker each day and I have become unable to endure this darkness any longer. I love you very much and what I'm about to do has nothing to do with you. I'm down at the creek under the old oak tree. I have timed my death so you could find me in time to donate my organs so I can bring some happiness into someone's world. If I could give a kidney to save a life or sight to someone going blind, my life would have had value. I cannot find happiness but I feel by being an organ donor, I can give happiness to someone else. Please do not be sad that I am gone; I'm just not strong enough to continue life's journey. Love, Allen"

Allen's mother immediately pulled out her cell phone and called 911. She then ran to where the big oak tree was and while she was running she heard a big splash. Panic filled her body and she took off her high heels so she could run faster. By the time she made it to the creek, Allen was floating on top of the water facedown. She ran into the water and pulled him out to the edge of the embankment but was unable to pull his body all the way out of the water. Her body became completely limp when she realized he was no longer breathing. When the ambulance arrived, Allen's mother cried out, "Please help me." One of the medics immediately began giving CPR but it was too late. Allen's mother told the medics that he wanted to be an organ donor. They immediately loaded his body into the ambulance. A police car drove up at this time and took Allen's mother with them to the hospital. She was given a sedative to calm her down. This event will change her life forever.

Allen's kidneys went to save a six-year-old boy's life. His parents took Allen's mother under their wings and made her a part of their son's life – a gift for a gift. By being a part of the six-year-old boy's life, Allen's mother was able to endure the loss of her son. I know she'll live with the thought that, at the last, Allen had thought about what he could do for others. Knowing he had a good thought before ending his own life helped her to live with what happened to her son. Allen's father became a recluse; he totally withdrew from life, retreating from the world to live in solitude. At least the boys who had bullied Allen seemed to recognize some of their guilt, and they became meek and submissive to everyone. They will have the blood of Allen on their hands for the rest of their lives. So many people's lives will be touched by this one event.

BreAnna was instrumental in helping me deal with Allen's death. I think BreAnna is filled with the Holy Spirit and has been given the gift of compassion to support those in dire need of healing of the soul. Maybe I just feel deeper than most people or maybe it was because I had played on the rope that went out over the pond at the wildlife refuge behind my house since I was a kid. Whatever the reason, BreAnna helped me deal with my emotions. When Brad fell into the pond at my party, I had been able to laugh and have fun with it. For a long time after Allen's death, every time I saw the rope, all I could think of was Allen. BreAnna made me see the light – that Allen had made a choice. We all have choices in life; we can make the most out of this precious gift God gave us or we can dwell in darkness. In this day and time, no one should put up with abuse. Allen could have called the Department of Human Services to stop his dad from abusing him. He could also have gone to the principal to report the bullying; he didn't do either one. Others should not have to pay the price if they are innocent of any malice toward Allen. BreAnna got this through my head and I was able to get past it all. It is so good to have BreAnna back in my life.

It also felt good to have Jake back in my life. He is going to fit in with my new set of friends because he and Kyle have so much in common. They are both freakin' geniuses who, I truly believe, will be changers for the better of the world we live in.

I remember Jake having me over to his house one day to show me his latest experiment to save the world from itself. He was growing plankton in tall glass tubes to be used as biofuels. Biofuels release less carbon dioxide than gasoline when burned. The type of carbon dioxide that plankton creates is the same carbon dioxide that plankton absorbs from the atmosphere when it grows. Jake told me how this could prevent global warming because of the release and capture cycle burning plankton would create.

He was also concerned about the future price of corn on the cob, his favorite vegetable. In his opinion, the government seems to be obsessed and preoccupied excessively with his ears of corn. They think that burning corn for fuel is the answer to global warming. Jake says why burn precious food on thousands of acres when all you have to do is capture plankton that people destroy in swimming pools. It just makes good sense.

If we make more plankton than can be used by automobiles then farmers could use the excess to improve land and soil so farmers could grow more ears of corn for Jake.

When Jake would show me his glass tubes with plankton he would talk about how photosynthesis occurs when plants take in energy from the sun and carbon dioxide from the atmosphere and turn them into oxygen and sugar. This is why he thinks that fossil fuels from plants rather than dinosaurs are the answer to the fuel shortage. He would talk about how the world will always need oil because it is the key raw material used for manufacturing of products such as artificial fibers for clothing, shampoos, deodorants, and all plastics.

Jake talked about ways to keep the plankton warm so it would continue to grow day and night. During the day, sunlight and solar panels would warm the tubes and at night he would put them underground and let the earth's geothermal power heat the plankton for continual growth. An automatic submergible pump would move the plankton into tubes deep within the earth. Geothermal energy can be harnessed through water piped underground. That water is heated from magma deep inside the earth. This would provide warm steam to keep the plankton growing.

Jake has a wealthy sponsor who has provided the materials for his experiment. I have high hopes that Jake will be instrumental in reversing global warming. He has a passion and a vision and a mind that is capable of transforming the ways things are done in today's world. The majority of people living in developing countries depend on corn as the basis of their food source. Jake says humanity shouldn't make fuels from food crops, especially corn. That is what I like so much about Jake; he will get up on his soapbox and show all sides of a situation. But then he will find something personal that a person, particularly himself, can relate to.

I have joy in my heart that is unexplainable due to the reunion of my best friends ever. I now feel like I'm part of their lives once again. Bringing my two sets of friends together by having a party was the best idea I ever had.

Chapter 10
A Summer Week at the Beach

I woke up to a bright and breezy morning. The sun was shining through my window and brightening up the glass of orange juice sitting on the nightstand. It is a special delight to have breakfast in bed with the sound and smell of the ocean filling my senses. This is my first time to have my own room in a hotel with room service and breakfast in bed. I feel so special and alive. My parents are in the room next to me, so I feel safe but free at the same time. The color of my room is blue like the ocean with off white trim, contrasting like the sand on the beach with the ocean. After finishing a hearty breakfast of bacon and eggs with cinnamon toast, I'm heading for the beach. My new bathing suit is a bright aqua with silver lining. It looks fabulous against my bronze skin. My beach attire is completed by my hat, which has a large floppy white brim with incredible sunray-preventing capabilities. My face is protected year round from any damaging effect of weather with sunscreen, hats, makeup or, as today, a combination of all three. My mother gives me marvelous advice on how to care for myself for the future. My shoes are sandals made from white hot rimstones. As I walk to the beach, my body is filled with wonderful feelings of sheer joy. I look amazing. My parents are still asleep and I have a miraculous feeling of freedom; after all, I'm fifteen and very mature, soon to be sixteen, on July 25. A year ago I would have been afraid to go anywhere by myself. It's astonishing how brave one can become in just one year.

However, as I approach the beach, the feeling of needing to cover my body with more clothes overwhelms me. My large wicker handbag has a beach towel, cut-off shorts and a tee shirt. I pull out my cut-offs and climb into them and I now feel secure again.

A white seagull flies right in front of my face and another feeling of alarm rushes through me. Although I have the feeling of being brave but fragile at the same time, I continue toward the ocean. After all, I'm fifteen and will be driving a car in a few days.

Even though it is early in the morning, people are setting up on the beach for the day. My feeling of being alone and not knowing anybody here takes me, yet again, in another direction. My comfort level will not let me join these people, at least not yet. I eased toward a cluster of palm trees because they gave me some cover. The beach is covered with sea shells of all different colors. The ocean water would wash up on the beach and ever so slightly move the shells to clean some and cover others up. The vastness of the ocean is truly magnificent. All the different colors bouncing in all directions is breathtaking. As I walk toward the water, it rolls in my direction. First, it covers my toes; then my ankles are covered with white frothy, foamy bubbles, and suddenly my knees are covered with aqua-colored ocean water. This is so cool. As fast as it rolled in, it rolled back out again. As I glanced out the vastness of the ocean, a large swell moving along the surface generated by either gravity or the wind was surging with velocity that only the ocean can deliver. I had taken only a few steps more toward the water when it receded, but it was quickly followed by the wave crashing against my body, which knocked my feet right out from under me. My whole body was surging in the direction of the middle of the ocean. As fast as it was pulling to the center, it released me and I was lying in the sand, wet from head to toe. I scrambled on my hands and knees to reach dry sand.

My heart was beating to a rhythm and pulsing amplitude I had never before experienced. I thought a heart attack was on me, but I soon realized it was lessening and that it was fear-spiked adrenaline that was the cause. My friends had teased me before I left home by saying, "Beware of the undertow." They told me the undertow would pull me out to the deep water and I would never return. They had been right and for a few scary moments I thought it was the end for me.

I grabbed my bag and headed for my room shaking like a leaf from fear. The warm sand was soothing to my feet and I could feel my composure returning. The safety of the hotel was only a few feet away and a welcoming sight. As I tried to put the key in the door, my hand was shaking so badly I had to use my other hand to steady it. After entering the room, all I wanted was to lock the door and crawl under the covers.

My mom knocked on my door and said, "Honey, when you're dressed, meet us at the café for a quick bite." I told her, "Sure, after I take a shower."

We had made plans to go parasailing in the afternoon. This is where a rope is attached to a boat at one end and to a parachute at the other end. When the boat takes off, the canopy attached by the harness catches wind and the person is lifted into the air. The boat pulls the person around the shore line, and when the boat stops, the person descends.

Guess who was first in line to go parasailing? Yours truly, of course. Two guys strapped me in and gave instructions on how to land. Then they motioned to the driver of the boat to take off. Before I could say, "I'm ready," my feet were off the ground and I was steadily going upward. This is truly an amazing feeling.

It's like being free as a bird. The higher in the sky, the quieter it got. It is by far the most peaceful and tranquil feeling I have ever experienced. The buildings looked like toys and the cars looked like ants.

The boat stopped for a moment and in a flash, the parachute began to descend. Then a breeze lifted it once again. It felt like a yoyo. Thoughts were running through my head about the rope breaking and the canopy being blown across the ocean until I could no longer see the shoreline. Then the wind would die down and the canopy would descend into a large group of aquatic animals known as sharks swimming together. Suddenly, the boat started running again and everything once again was smooth. Once my heart stopped hammering in my chest, I remembered the instructions given prior to takeoff. If you want to go left, pull on the left side of the harness, and the same principle applies for going right. You do this when the boat stops. This time, when the boat stopped, I pulled a hard left and began to descend to the shoreline right into the arms of the guys who strapped me in. One of the guys said, "Good job. For awhile, we thought you were going to stay up there." I told them that I had forgotten what to do when the boat stopped, temporarily. It came to me after the jerking started and I thought the rope might break and I would wind up in the middle of the ocean. They got a good laugh out of that.

After that little adventure, it was time for lunch. My parents had arranged to have lunch on a boat and afterwards we would do some fishing. Lunch consisted of sea bass grilled with onions, bell peppers and garlic. The salad was a leaf lettuce topped with tomatoes and a balsamic vinegar dressing. The warm wheat bread topped with butter melted in my mouth. This was a perfect lunch for someone who had just had visions of being lunch for a bunch of sharks. I took a deep breath and let everyone know how good lunch was, asked to be excused and went topside to take a nap.

I woke up to my mother's scream, which was a loud piercing cry for help. She was hysterical and had blood all over her blouse. I ran in her direction and at the same time saw my dad lying on the deck drenched in his own blood and a very large swordfish also on the deck flopping around in a rage. I screamed for help and one of the owners of the boat immediately started stabbing this fish with a long pole. Once the swordfish was dying, we rushed to my dad, wrapped his leg with a belt to stop the bleeding. He said he was okay and then asked, "If you would be so kind as to put my swordfish on ice so we can have him for supper, I will be one happy camper." Dad was trying to calm us down with his humor. We appreciated his comical nature but he was getting weak and his skin was very pale. The captain of the boat called for an emergency helicopter to pick him up from the boat. He let them know he had a serious situation urgently requiring prompt action. The captain knew he needed to keep my dad awake, so he was grilling him on how this fish managed to stab him in the leg. My dad told his fish story about how he fought tooth and nail to get this swordfish into the boat by himself, which he did, and how it was uncontrollable once he landed him. He talked about how he had never seen a fish so strong out of water, and how the sword on the end of that fish felt like a razor. The captain was doing a great job with my dad and suddenly the Coast Guard arrived with a medic on board. They pulled up next to our boat and jumped on. The medic had an IV bag and began to puncture dad's arm to administer a glucose drip. He let us know it was necessary to stabilize dad before the helicopter arrived. They began to clean out the hole the fish had made in his leg. The medic told us it had hit a vein and that was why there was so much blood. He wrapped a bandage tightly around the wound and then checked my dad's eyes with a light. By this time, the helicopter was in sight and the medic was loading dad on a stretcher. The helicopter lowered its cable, which was quickly attached, and dad was lifted into the belly of the helicopter and off they went. The Coast Guard offered to take us to shore so we could get to the hospital emergency room. We loaded up and off we went. I did not know it was possible to move this fast on water. The Coast Guard guy explained to me and my mom that the helicopter was a much smoother ride for my dad as well as much faster. My mom was praising them for doing such a good job and then she began to cry. They assured her that her husband was going to be fine.

When we got to the hospital we rushed to the emergency room and were told my dad was stable and the doctor was in the process of stitching up the wound. My mom began to cry again; I grabbed her hand and she hugged my neck and said, "I'm so glad he's all right that I can't help but cry." Our emotions were so high that I began to cry as well. The doctor came out of the room and said we could come in to see him. We dried our eyes and went into his room.

He was sitting up in his bed smiling. Our eyes were red, so he knew we had been crying. He said, "You two come here and give me a hug. The Doc said that swordfish nicked a vein in my leg and that's why there was so much blood. I'm going to be fine. The Doc said I can go home in about four hours. Just in time to cook fish for dinner." About that time, the captain entered the room. He said, "Yes, he will be a tasty fish at that. I have him on ice. Glad to see you are okay." Mother said, "It will be my pleasure to fry that fish after what he did." Dad got a kick out of that.

Mom left to escort the captain to their room to put half the fish in the freezer. Mom and dad's room had a small kitchen because they had anticipated a fish fry. Things are working out pretty much as planned, although some extraordinary events had not been part of the original plan.

I stayed with my dad in the hospital to comfort him. As I covered his feet with a blanket, he dozed off. Thoughts ran through my mind how I would be the one who had something bad happen. I've heard of premonitions, a forewarning of the future, but never put much stock in them. Now I think this will be something to which I will give more thought. Nature gives animals this sense so maybe people have more of it than what they want to admit to knowing.

Dad started talking in his sleep and I think he was talking to that fish. He kept saying, "You're a good fighter, but you're mine. I'm cooking dinner tonight and you're it." He would thrash around in the bed like he was fighting for his life. Suddenly, he woke up. At the same time mother walked into the room. Mother was telling dad how she and the captain cleaned the swordfish and put half in the freezer and the other half would be for supper. She let him know he was getting his color back and she was taking him back to the hotel in one hour. Dad asked mom and me to come close to the side of his bed and he put his arm around our necks and started apologizing for putting a damper on our vacation. We all started crying because of the realization he could actually have bled to death.

The doctor came into the room and said, "I didn't mean to interrupt but I have crutches to aid in walking while you are healing." My dad said, "Thanks for everything; I will return the crutches before flying home." The doctor shook hands with each of us and wished us good luck on the rest of our stay. Dad was released and we headed for the hotel. He lay down and was out like a light. Mother began preparing dinner and I set the table with paper plates and plastic cups and forks. I was famished from this very eventful day. This fish is going to be just the comfort food I need.

The food is on our plates, the drink is in our glasses and it's time to wake up dad to join us for dinner. Mom said his name four times before he finally woke up. The smell of fish fried in a cornmeal batter filled the room. We all smiled at each other and took a bite.

Mom told me the next morning that she was going to stay in with dad but if I wanted to play on the beach I had her blessing. Well, I certainly did not want to spend the rest of my vacation in my room, so I took her up on it. I grabbed my things and headed out the door. Familiarity with the beach has lessened my fears. This time I walk in amongst all the people on the beach and pick a spot near the water, spread my towel out and start applying sunscreen. The warm sun on my legs and back was energizing. It's time for a dip in the ocean. Instead of fear of being around people, they are now welcomed after the last couple of days. The old saying, there is safety in numbers, now has meaning for me.

As I walk into the water, the sweet sound of children laughing is refreshing. They have a large colorful beach ball bouncing off their hands and heads. One of the kids hit the ball in my direction and I bounce it back to them. As I swim further into the ocean, the kids get older and older until there are teenagers all around me. Instead of a beach ball, they are playing with Frisbees – a disk-like plastic toy that players throw and catch. A Frisbee was being carried through the air by the wind and floated right into my hands. The game these teens are playing is wide open for anyone who wants to participate. All you have to do is catch and throw - no questions asked. Because this area of the beach has many motels and hotels, most of these teens don't know each other; they're all on vacation and from places all over the United States. That puts all of us on the same playing field; nobody really knows anybody, so there are no predispositions as to who to spend time with. It will be exciting to meet and spend time with new people.

A total of nine teens ranging from about 13 to 17 years of age are engaging in this Frisbee game with intense enthusiasm, physical over-activity and competition. There is no scorekeeping, but when the Frisbee is caught when no one thought it possible, everyone cheers. There is something about salt water that gives buoyancy when you jump up to catch the Frisbee. It is a dense capacity that allows you to float without effort and rise higher when you jump.

Each time someone caught the Frisbee, they returned it immediately to a waiting group of teens. One of the guys jumped so high to catch it, when he came back down he made a splash that had those too close drinking salt water. I saw something in this guy I admired – competitiveness. This guy seemed to come closer and closer until we were side by side. He said, "Where are you from?" I pointed to my hotel and he said, "No, I mean what state." "I'm from Oklahoma – Tahlequah." He splashed me in the face with water and said, "I went to a football game where an Oklahoma team beat a Texas team and I'm from Texas and my big brother is a receiver." I laughed, splashed him back and told him, "Oklahoma is known for their football programs." As we talked, he became less aggressive and so we didn't splash each other in the face anymore. He had a great smile and was very attractive. It was time to find out this guy's name; since he's not volunteering to tell me, I'll have to ask. He was really into this Frisbee game and was drifting away so I yelled, "What's your name?" He replied, "Jeff." I called back, "Mine is Chelsea."

The game went on for another hour and I decided to go on shore and soak up some sun. After I dried off and put on some lotion, I covered my face and lay down on my towel to relax. As I drifted off to sleep, I heard my name, looked up and there was Jeff with his towel. "Can I join you," he said. I said, "Sure."

We talked about what a great beach we are on and how warm the water has been. Jeff began telling me about how he had gone snorkeling and had seen fish he did not even know existed. He talked about how close they came to his mask and about reaching out and touching them before they would scurry away and swirl around just out of reach. He talked about how life on earth started in the ocean and some of these creatures have been around millions of years. He told me that snorkeling should be on my list of things to do before I went home. It's like a zoo of ocean creatures all around you that are curious as to what you are. Somehow, they know you don't belong.

I let Jeff do most of the talking because I was still a little upset and distracted after dad's scenario with that very tasty fish. He then suggested we take a walk on the beach and look for shells, which I thought was a great idea, so off we went. We must have picked up 20 shells when Jeff picked up a shell that had a perfectly round hole on the end of it. He gave it to me and said if I ran a chain or string through it, I could wear it as a necklace. This was a great idea; it could be a keepsake from Jeff and a memento to remind me of this great vacation. I took it, thanked him and we went on in search of more shells.

As we walked along the beach kicking up sand, Jeff let me know we were taking the homes of crabs and snails. I never gave it much thought before, but he was right. Nevertheless, I did not put any of them back. I fully intended to put them in my aquarium at home.

I noticed by the sun's position it was getting late and I told Jeff I needed to mosey on down to the hotel because my parents would be worried about me. At this time, he let me know a volleyball game had been scheduled for noon tomorrow and pointed at a net on the beach. I told him I would check with my parents as to their plans.

Beach volleyball sounds like a blast. With a competitive nature when it comes to sports, an athletic body with physically strong legs and arms (which are a requirement for beach volleyball) I said to myself, "Look out; I'm coming."

Mom and dad had watched TV all day while dad was trying to regain his strength. His leg was all bruised up and he was still using the crutches. Looks like beach volleyball tomorrow plus an opportunity to sleep in a little later.

The smell of ocean salt water and the sound of waves

breaking on the beach were like a soothing song intended to lull you to sleep. I lay in my bed and thanked God for letting my dad be okay and for the great time I was having on this vacation. Thoughts of all my friends back home were running through my head as well, and I thanked God for them also.

Morning came crashing through my window and sleeping in just wasn't in the cards for today. I knocked on my parents' door and offered to fix breakfast for them. There were no arguments. Breakfast will consist of orange juice and toasted bagels with cinnamon and raisins plus cut up melons. This should be energy packed but light enough to give me staying power for the volleyball game with my new friend, Jeff. Mom said to have a fun day because she would be staying in for another day with dad. Hopefully, he would be better tomorrow.

After breakfast, it was time to get my swimsuit on and find a string for the sea shell Jeff found for me on the beach. My first choice was a shoe string from one of dad's shoes. The hole in the shell was too small for that option. After giving intense thought to this matter, an idea popped into my head. Dental floss is small and yet strong enough to hold the shell. Perfect is the word I'm looking for. I tied it in a bow to give it some style. I pulled my hair back with a rubber band and tied a wide white ribbon around it. I'm ready to put my game face on and hit the beach.

Out the door I went. The beach was filling up. After a few steps, I remembered I'd forgotten my water bottle. I turned to return to my room and heard Jeff call my name. I turned back and said, "I'll be right there; I forgot something." It was so good to hear his voice; it made it easier to walk to the net.

When I came out my door, Jeff grabbed my hand and started running toward the net. He let me know that our team was warming up and learning each member's strengths and weaknesses. He asked me what my strengths were and I told him I was extremely strong and had good hand/eye coordination. Then he asked what my weaknesses were. I told him I was not as tall as most of players, but that I could jump high and that would help make up for being so short.

Even though the game doesn't start until noon and it's only 10:00 a.m., our whole team was already assembled around the net. They had already agreed on a name for the team before I was asked to join them; they had chosen Beach Bums. I had never thought of myself as a bum, but I guess it will grow on me. Our opponents called themselves The Barefooters. Our team had four players and The Barefooters had five, but two of their players were younger. None of us had ever been on a volleyball team so no one officially knew how to keep score, so we made up the rules as we went. Everyone had heard of a net ball, but no one knew what to do with it, so we all decided to just ignore it when it happened. The boundary would be lines drawn in the sand. Points would be made when a team was unable to return the ball over the net or if the ball went outside the boundary lines.

We were still waiting for two of The Barefooters to arrive, so everyone decided to take a dip in the ocean while we waited. Jeff was walking with me and made mention he really liked my necklace. I responded by saying a really nice guy gave it to me. He just smiled, grabbed my hand and started running toward the water. Before I knew it, the water was chin high. I felt so good. Jeff told me to try floating on my back. He said because of the salt water, it would not require much effort. He was so right. It felt like I was suspended on the surface of water without sinking, like being on a float.

The other two Barefooters were coming down the beach and soon everyone was in the water. They yelled out, "It's not noon yet and we want a dip in the water." They came running in and joined us. One of them said, "The losers of the beach volleyball game have to buy soft drinks after the game." Jeff said, "You're on."

After a good splash in the water it was time for the game between the Beach Bums and the Barefooters to begin. We tossed a coin to see who would serve the first ball. Looks like Jeff is going to start the game because he won the toss.

This game is such a blast. I become very good at spiking the ball where there was no way our opponents could return it. After a while they figured out our weak spot and after that I seldom received the ball. But that's okay because when it was my turn to serve the ball, I hit their weak spot every time. This went on until the score of 20 points was reached. In the end, there was only a two-point difference in our scores. The Barefooters won. Let's not forget the Beach Bums only had four team players while the Barefooters had five.

One and all, we enjoyed our soft drinks. No one was out for blood in this game - just fun. There is something refreshing about a bunch of teens getting together and all speaking the same language. We may all have different values but we still understand each other. Teens have all this energy and we find ways to release it, both physically and mentally. This little group of volleyball players also has a special way of exercising their mental muscles. They draw straws and the one with the short straw has to tell a personal story. This is their way of getting to know each other better. Today seemed to be Jeff's lucky day; not only did he win the toss but he got the short straw. This is going to be fun because although I don't know a lot about Jeff, I just know there is something about him I like.

Jeff began by introducing me to this group of teens, most of whom come to this beach every summer. Then he went on to tell me about the tradition they have of drawing straws every summer, and the short-straw recipients have to tell a story of something in their life that has had a positive impact on them. Jeff's story began with a trip to the doctor because of muscle cramps. Jeff is very muscular but had a problem of not having enough potassium in his body to feed these well-developed muscles. The doctor suggested he eat more bananas and pears. Of the two choices for improving his health, Jeff's preference was for pears. Because they are about three times more expensive than bananas, his mother had suggested he plant a pear tree. The tree only cost $7.00 but produced $100.00 worth of pears during its first year of producing pears and as it grew bigger the next year, it produced $300 worth of pears. Jeff's mother canned these pears so he could enjoy them all year long. Jeff talked about what a valuable lesson this has been for him. He talked about the gratification he received watching the sapling grow and produce fruit that he would eat to nourish his muscles and stop the cramps. What a process!

Wow, what a story! Now I know what it is about him; he thinks about this thing called life a lot like I do. Take care of your body and it will take care of you. He vibrates at the same frequency that I do. I feel the connection between us so strongly that my energy level is the highest I have ever experienced. I've only known this guy for two days, so how could this be happening?

After Jeff told his story, everyone clapped their hands; some shouted "Good job," while others said, "More." Jeff said, "Enough already," and started walking toward me. He grabbed my hand and we started walking toward the ocean. Jeff started talking about what a great group of teens these guys were and how he looked forward every year to vacation so he could be with them again. He talked about how different this group was compared to the average teen. Many teens are rebellious and somewhat self-destructive while this group has chosen to focus on what they can do to improve their lives physically, mentally and spiritually. Each has set a goal to become a centenarian – a person 100 years old or older – and still be in good health. He explained how you can enjoy most of what life has to offer as long as it is done in moderation. That is the secret to good health. "Members of our group," he explained, "make it a point to share some experience that has had a positive impact on their lives and share it."

Jeff started talking about his older brother who had a problem with drugs. He talked about how he started out just having fun with them and, next thing you know, he was a full-blown addict. He talked about how some of these drugs are so potent that with just a few times of using them you can become an addict. In talking with his brother, it had become clear that ordinary life had no meaning for him; all he could think about was his next time to get high. Jeff looked at me and said, "Can you imagine not looking forward to vacation, or not looking forward to seeing your friends? What kind of life is that when all you want is a room and your drugs?"

Jeff's eyes seemed so sad as he talked about the loss of his brother. It was a loss because, although his brother was still living, he could not care less whether Jeff was dead or alive; all he cared about was his next fix. Jeff talked about how his group made plans to change the way teens are being attracted to the darker side of life. He talked about how the dark side had nothing to offer but death and destruction. He told me his brother was only 22 years old but looked 40 already. The drugs owned him and reclaiming his freedom from drugs meant nothing to him.

I thought effecting such change would be a marvelous thing to do for mankind if, indeed, these teens could set a new way of growing up, being hip and still be the generation of centenarians. I told Jeff, "When I get back home, your cause will become a tradition in Oklahoma. This game of drawing straws is fixing to become very popular there, too."

It was getting late in the afternoon and I told Jeff I needed to go spend some time with my parents but hoped I would be able to see him tomorrow. Jeff said, "We're renting surf boards tomorrow around noon and you are invited to join us." I gave him a thumb's up and headed off for my room. I really needed a shower – playing beach volleyball gets sand all over you.

Mom and dad had been in their room all day and were getting restless. Mom knocked on my door and asked if I wanted to join them for dinner in town. I opened the door and told her I was just about ready to knock on their door to make that very suggestion. I knew Dad needs to get out and get some fresh air and I'm glad it was their idea because I'm not much for pushing my ideas on anyone.

The restaurant sat on a pier, which is a platform extending from a shore over water and supported by piles or pillars used to secure it so it won't wash out into the ocean. We got a table next to a window and it generated the sense of sitting right on the water. I gazed out the window and reminisced on the days of this wonderful vacation. I thought about my parents and felt awful about the fish incident. Then I thought about the new friendships with an incredible group of intellectual, rational rather than emotional, teens I had met on the beach. Life is good.

Dad asked what looked good on the menu and I replied, "Steak and baked potatoes with wheat rolls." He said, "Sounds good to me; I'll have the same." Dad still looks a little pale and weak, but he is trying to have a good time. I feel sorry for him. He asked, "Are you having a good time, Chelsea? It's important to me that this vacation is fun for you." I replied, "Dad, you have no idea how much fun this vacation is. I have met the coolest bunch of teens. Their goal is to become centenarians." He said, "I haven't even seen them, but I like their philosophy. Wisdom by intellectual investigation along with moral self-discipline will definitely put you on the road to becoming a centenarian. Would you say they meet those standards?" I said, "Absolutely, definitely, without a doubt! That describes their philosophy.

They are into eating healthy, feeding their spirits with high morals and educating their minds about what not to do that would harm the body." Dad said, "This is great. I would like to meet these kids. They sound like aliens to me – creatures from outer space. Do they have large almond-shaped eyes with really small bodies?" I laughed and said, "No. They may not be your typical teens since their goals are to change the self-destructive nature of teens that can lead to ruinous results in their lives. By the way, we are going surfing tomorrow, if you would like to watch." Dad said, "I might just take you up on that." Mom said, "Can I watch, too?" I said, "You bet!"

I had a great time with my parents and could tell they were tickled to death that I was having a delightful time. I don't know if they will come to the beach and watch us surf, but I so hope they will. I understand that they get a big kick out of seeing me have fun.

The next morning I woke up before the sun rose. It must be that my body knew this is the last day of my vacation and it's time to have as much fun as I can. I think that breakfast in bed for my parents is a good way to start the day. I decided to start with blueberry bagels with cream cheese and a half a cantaloupe. A pot of coffee and fresh strawberries topped off the breakfast. They both gave me a big hug and told me they hoped I would catch a big wave. I told them that I hoped to see them on the beach and that a little sun would do both of them some good.

It felt good to spend some time with my parents and I could tell they enjoyed my company. Family is the most important thing in my life because I know they will always be there for me. Some day I will create my own family and I want them to know that I will always be there for them. Friends are great and bring about instant joy to a teens life, but friends come and go while family is forever.

It's time to hit the beach and catch a wave. Today,

I'm the early bird and the first to hit the water. It feels like the great big ocean belongs to me. I made a game out of diving head first into the waves to see if I could be stronger than the break of the wave, but no such luck. Each time, I was pushed back toward the shore. Water is a very powerful force.

I heard my name called, and turned to see Jeff waving at me. I let the wave take me in to shore. Body surfing is great but now it's time for the real thing – board surfing.

As I walked on to the shore, Jeff grabbed my hand and said, "Let's go pick out our boards. What's your favorite color?" I replied, "Pink."

There were lots of boards to choose from and I found one that was black with pink flowers on it. Jeff chose a pure yellow board. We waxed them down thoroughly so our feet would be able to grab the boards. Jeff gave me some pointers on how to stay up on the board; he said it is all in the balance. He recommended I use my arms to help balance my body and bend my knees ever so slightly to make my body like a spring. "If you can ride a skate board, you can surf," Jeff said. I told him that I can roller skate and he repeated, "It's all about balance and that should help." After the boards were waxed, we put them in the water, laid on top of them and paddled out into the ocean. It was a perfect day and the waves were breaking high. It was fun just riding the waves on our bellies.

All Jeff's friends were paddling ahead of us since they already knew how to surf. Jeff was taking it slow with me because I was his student and he wanted me to ace the first wave. My confidence was at an all time high as Jeff instructed me to plant my feet on the board in a way that I could balance my body with my arms. He had me stay in a squatted position until I got the feel of the wave. I would go from squatting to standing to squatting depending on what the wave was doing. This is flippin' great. I own this wave and Jeff is watching me closely with a pleased smile on his face. Jeff's friends went out further into the ocean but were catching up to us by squatting to pick up speed. Suddenly they were all around us. It was thrilling to have them cut across the water right in front of me. I got several thumb's ups. The group energy was simply amazing. This is the best day of my vacation. I feel like a natural surfer; like this is in my bones deep in the core of my body.

As we near the shore we all zigzag around each other like a school of fish. It was amazing, as if we could actually read each others' moves. When on shore, everyone agreed that I was a natural and wanted me to go out further into the ocean with them. I said, "Let's go," and off we went. Jeff stayed close, but had full confidence in my ability to ride the big wave. We could hardly see the shoreline and that meant it was time to mount the surf board. This wave was definitely a whole new level from where I started. My stomach was full of butterflies from the anticipation as my feet were planted on the board. As I raised my body to ride the wave of my life, it was as if I was one with the wave. The wave was carrying me on its back and guiding me into the shore. My knees were slightly bent and I used my arms for balance, by holding them out like wings on a bird. The water below my surfboard was crystal clear and I could see a dolphin swimming beside my board as if he were trying to race me. I shifted my body to the right to see if this great marine mammal would follow me and, sure enough, he did. It was as if this dolphin was playing with me. He looked me right in the eye and started swimming circles around my surfboard. It was thrilling and, as if a sudden intense emotion filled my body, I began quivering and trembling with excitement. I could not stop smiling.

This wave is huge and the ride is one of a lifetime. Jeff was watching over me like I was his responsibility if something went wrong. That was a good feeling to know he cared enough to focus on me instead of the wave. What a great guy! My buddy, the dolphin, is now in front of my surfboard leading me into shore. The huge wonderful wave gets smaller and smaller as we get closer to the shoreline. Suddenly, the dolphin jumps out of the water and darts back into the ocean to catch the next big wave. I waved goodbye as if he would know what it meant. Jeff was watching and I was so glad he had seen my dolphin. Before I knew it, I was back on shore and Jeff was telling me what a natural surfer I am. Each of his friends gave me an air high five and said, "Good job!" I was so excited and it showed all over my face.

The gang started to get in a huddle and Jeff grabbed my hand and put me right in the middle. He said, "Let's hear it for Chelsea." They shouted, "Way to go, Chelsea." Then Jeff began to explain to me that normally we would draw straws for someone to give the meaning of a large word that they think would be beneficial in the future. Instead of drawing straws, Jeff recommended to the gang that I give a word that I thought would be appropriate. I agreed and gave the word, fundamental, which is another word for basic or an essential part. An example is fundamental principles or basic principles. The gang gave their approval of the new word and another high five was in order.

Jeff grabbed my hand and off we went in the direction of our beach towels. Jeff knew we were running out of time and that I would soon be on a plane heading for home and he wanted to spend some one-on-one time. He gave me his email address and invited me to visit his MySpace page. In return I gave him my webpage that lists, "Eleven Teenage Guidelines." It must be fate that brought us together because we both want to make teenagers' lives better. The teen years are very awkward for some teens and to be guided through the difficult years could save them future distress.

This time I grabbed Jeff's hand and told him I had to catch a plane for home and I wanted him to walk me to my room. I told him what a great time I had with him and his friends and that I would email him when I got home. He let me know he was looking forward to our continued love/friendship. We then said our goodbyes.

Mom and dad had already packed for me to make sure we wouldn't be late for the plane. Almost before I knew it, I was on a plane reminiscing about my new friend and the fun and love I'd had with him and all his and now my vacation friends. Next I glanced over at my mom and dad and saw how dad's near-death experience made them somehow closer. I felt a big smile come across my face as I fell into a slumber.

THE END

Guidance For Teens

1) Live in the moment; that is when life's most precious times are.

2) Harness your jealousy; don't punish others for your shortcomings.

3) Don't carry bad memories like a ball and chain; let them go.

4) Dwell on the good things and not the bad things in life.

5) Love yourself and others will love you back.

6) Remember how to listen.

7) Friends don't make friends feel stupid.

8) Respect yourself – don't harm your body or mind.

9) Make your own history, one you can be proud of. You can never get this day back so make the most of it.

10) Don't lie to yourself; always have the facts.

11) Your values are your blueprint; stick to them. You live with your values until you die, so stick by your values.

References

1) Riverside Webster's II New College Dictionary

2) Holy Bible

3) Constitution of the United States

www.ingramcontent.com/pod-product-compliance
Lightning Source LLC
Chambersburg PA
CBHW020626250626
47154CB00004B/1690